With a sickening crunch of metal, the huge silver truck rammed Joaquin's vehicle from behind...

The squad car lunged forward, and he struggled to keep it on the road. Luann held her seat belt so hard her hands were turning white. Joaquin slammed his foot down on the accelerator.

A shot suddenly rang out, cracking the car's rear window.

"Get down!" Joaquin shouted. He pulled out his own weapon, but it was all he could do to keep a few feet ahead of the aggressive driver behind them.

Another shot sounded, and Joaquin heard a large bang as his left rear tire blew. His heart clenched as the truck slammed into them again, pushing them towards the ditch. He looked for his gun, but it had fallen on the floor out of reach.

Luann cried out in fear and Joaquin grabbed her hand, knowing that this act of comfort may very well be his last. They were mere seconds from death...

Kathleen Tailer is an operations manager and attorney serving in the Office of the State Courts Administrator for the Supreme Court of Florida. She earned a law degree from Florida State University and a BA from the University of New Mexico. Kathleen is a proud mother of eight children, five of whom she and her husband adopted. A passionate photographer and drummer, she also enjoys exploring new places and immersing herself in different cultures.

Books by Kathleen Tailer

Love Inspired Suspense

Under the Marshal's Protection
The Reluctant Witness
Perilous Refuge
Quest for Justice
Undercover Jeopardy
Perilous Pursuit
Deadly Cover-Up
Everglades Escape
Held for Ransom
Covert Takedown
Alaskan Wilderness Murder
Marked to Die
Showdown in the Rockies
Surviving the Desert
Missing in New Mexico

Visit the Author Profile page at LoveInspired.com for more titles.

MISSING IN NEW MEXICO

KATHLEEN TAILER

LOVE INSPIRED SUSPENSE
INSPIRATIONAL ROMANCE

MIX
Paper | Supporting responsible forestry
FSC® C021394
www.fsc.org

LOVE INSPIRED® SUSPENSE
INSPIRATIONAL ROMANCE

Recycling programs for this product may not exist in your area.

ISBN-13: 978-1-335-91919-9

Missing in New Mexico

For questions and comments about the quality of this book, please contact us at CustomerService@Harlequin.com.

Love Inspired
22 Adelaide St. West, 41st Floor
Toronto, Ontario M5H 4E3, Canada
www.LoveInspired.com

HarperCollins Publishers
Macken House, 39/40 Mayor Street Upper,
Dublin 1, D01 C9W8, Ireland
www.HarperCollins.com

Printed in Lithuania

1 2 3 4 5 6 7 8 9 10 LIT 28 27 26 25

Be strong and of a good courage, fear not, nor be afraid of them: for the LORD thy God, he it is that doth go with thee; he will not fail thee, nor forsake thee.

—*Deuteronomy* 31:6

For our wonderful church family,
our missionary friends in Africa and Israel,
and our amazing neighbors in Shell Point, Florida.
Thank you for your love and kindness.

Also for Suzy Harrington, Luann Tammany,
Janet Cubbage and Mary Ellen Cunningham,
who have all shown incredible resilience,
inner strength and devotion to God.
I am blessed to have you in my life and love you all.

I also continue to be blessed by
my wonderful family: Jim, James, Bethany, Daniel,
Keandra, Jessica, Nathan, Anna, Megan, Joshua O.,
Bradley, Brayden, B.J., Sophia, Stanley and Lilly.
Also in loving memory of our son, Joshua Evan Tailer,
who will forever be in our hearts.

And don't forget our fur babies:
Casey, Cocoa and Chloe...

ONE

Her brakes weren't working.

Fear swept over Luann St. John as she pumped the brakes again on the small rental sedan. It was a virtually new car—she shouldn't be having any sort of problem with the vehicle. She'd noticed the brakes were feeling a bit squishy when she first started driving this morning, but she'd thought that the unusual touch was just because they didn't quite feel the same as her normal car. She had also been so focused on her objective that she hadn't been paying attention to anything else. Now, however, a warning light flashed on the dashboard and the brake pedal was definitely getting less and less responsive. The facts were indisputable. She was careening down the twisting mountain road incredibly fast, and gravity was working against her as she quickly descended out of control.

She couldn't stop.

She couldn't even slow down. With each turn, her tires squealed against the pavement, her car tilted precariously, and her fear increased exponentially. She pressed the brake pedal so hard her foot started aching, but over and over again, she got the same response. Nothing. The pedal went straight to the floorboard, and if anything, the car accelerated as she headed fearfully into the next turn.

Panic gripped her heart. Now what? The mountain road was curvy all the way back to Del Norte, New Mexico, with granite boulders and thick forest on one side and a large drop-off on the other side into a huge drainage ditch designed to catch the mountain's runoff during the rare desert storms. There was a small guardrail on a couple of the turns, but most of the road and bends were unadorned, with nothing to keep her small car from plunging into the gully below.

Her mind felt frozen, and adrenaline pulsed through her body, making her muscles ache as she gripped the steering wheel. What should she do? Like a flash, inspiration hit her and she grabbed the emergency brake between the two seats and pulled the handle up hard with her right hand. Instead of stopping the car, however, the car made a grinding sound in the back and the small vehicle fishtailed into a radical spin. Time seemed to move in slow motion as Luann felt the car sliding across the ground and she fought to stay on the pavement. She screamed as the car careened across the road out of control, crossed the shoulder and then started falling. Seconds later, the car landed hard in the dry arroyo bed. A plume of dust and smoke billowed above the vehicle as it slowly tilted and came to rest at an awkward angle on its side with the driver's door wedged against the hard-packed earth. Airbags engaged upon impact, both from the dashboard and from the side doors, and the acrid smell of burned rubber filled the air.

Luann took a minute to regroup, then another as she struggled to calm her breathing and do a mental inventory of her aches and pains. She was alive, so regardless of the final outcome, she was already counting herself blessed. She pushed the airbag out of the way and gingerly lifted her fingers to touch her brow that was wet and sticky. She grimaced and drew back when she saw the blood that coated her fingers. Her head was pounding and her body felt sore all over, but she doubted the head injury was serious. Head wounds always bled a ridiculous amount, and hopefully a butterfly bandage or two would fix her up.

Her mind started spinning. She had survived the crash, but would anybody find her and be able to help her get back to town? She'd only seen one other car on the road so far, and she was in such a remote location she doubted anyone had seen or heard the accident. Now her car was probably well hidden in the arroyo. She wasn't even from this area of New Mexico. Would anybody realize she was missing and think to look for her?

There was no knight in shining armor mounted on a white palfrey riding in to save her. She had to save herself. She asked God for strength, then carefully studied the driver's-side door. It was jammed tightly against a wall of dirt, and there was no way she could get out, even through the window. There just wasn't enough space for her body to fit. She took a deep breath and considered her position. Her shoulder hurt where the seat belt had held her in place, and her left shoe seemed stuck between the metal of the car's frame and the dashboard that had been pushed forward into her lap. She released her seat belt and moved her foot gingerly and was finally able to disengage it from the metal trap. With a sigh of gratitude, she stretched out her foot. Her toes and ankle were still moving, and nothing felt broken.

She thought about yelling for help but instantly discarded the idea. If someone did happen to drive by, they would be focusing on the road, and most people usually had their windows up, especially now since it was late October and already getting colder outdoors. Even her own windows had been tightly shut to keep out the frigid wind. Other drivers wouldn't hear her cries, no matter how loudly she yelled, and she would probably just end up with a pounding headache even worse than what she already had.

She considered her location. The city of Tijeras lay to the west and was a much larger venue, but she was a good twenty miles away from the outskirts. She was staying in the tiny village of Del Norte, and it was only a few miles to the northeast. Her best bet was probably getting out of this undriveable car and to start walking in that direction, despite the cold. Del Norte barely registered on the map, and few people seemed to come down this rural mountain road that she had taken, but hopefully someone would drive by and offer her a ride if they saw her walking. Del Norte's population was under 4000, and according to the website, the area only boasted two bed-and-breakfasts, four restaurants, two gas stations, a pharmacy in the back of a small grocery store and a few other tourist shops, most of which featured the work of some of the local artists. A few were painters and sculptors, but the area was better known for the silver-and-turquoise jewelry that the residents designed and sold both online and through the tiny shops. There were also a handful of ranches nearby, and one in particular that featured trail rides and wilderness camping had garnered her interest.

Luann relaxed awkwardly against the seat, once again trying to gather her thoughts. She'd come to this small town in New Mexico on the eastern back of the Sandia Mountains to find out the truth about her father's disappearance. No, it was more than that. She was on a quest—to prove her father's innocence. She also wanted, somehow, to conquer the feelings of abandonment that had heavily impacted every adult relationship she'd ever had. Her father's disappearance had affected her in more ways than she'd ever really admitted, and she was only recently coming to realize that. But now it was time to face these issues head-on and start moving forward. This car accident was a bump in the road, but it wasn't going to deter her. Somehow, she would make lemonade out of these lemons and continue with her investigation.

She turned her thoughts back to her current predicament and maneuvered the best she could to pull her legs up and underneath her, then pushed her body toward the passenger's-side door. The engine had turned off as a result of the crash, and when she reached the button on the handle and pushed it to open the window, nothing happened, even though the key was still in the ignition. The door itself was jammed closed and refused to budge, no matter how hard she pushed against it. She paused a moment and blew a stray hair out of her eyes, then looked around the inside of the car for something—anything—that would help her get out of the car. Inspiration hit and she pulled the headrest out of the passenger seat, flipped it, and started hitting the two metal ends against the window. The safety glass shattered on the third hit, breaking into hundreds of tiny pieces. She ran the headrest around the window frame, cleaning away the remaining glass, careful to protect her skin from the sharp fragments. Sweat was already mixing with the blood on her brow, despite the cool air that rushed in, and she wiped it away with her sleeve to keep the moisture out of her eyes.

Once the glass was gone, she pitched the headrest behind her, found her purse and tossed it out of the car, and pulled herself up and out through the window. As soon as her legs were free, she slid toward the back of the rear fender and then jumped to get away from the vehicle. Heat emanated from the bottom of the car, and she enjoyed it for a moment, then studied the wall of the arroyo as she secured her purse strap across her chest. She was still sore in several places, but nothing felt broken, and the only thing bleeding was her head wound. That was a blessing. A few butterfly bandages and she'd be as good as new.

But why had her brakes failed in the first place? She was not mechanical by any means, but the car the rental company had provided was less than a year old. It was small and no-frills and should have been reliable.

Questions spun in her mind. Had someone tampered with her brakes? A cold chill swept down her spine as she considered the possibility.

If so, why? Her father's disappearance had occurred over twenty years ago. Who would care that she was asking questions this late after the event?

She thought back over what she knew of the case to date.

Twenty years ago, her father, Henry St. John, had disappeared with over two million dollars' worth of diamonds from his job at a well-established jewelry shop in

Las Cruces, New Mexico. Neither he nor the diamonds had ever been seen again. Luann had only been eight years old at the time, and her father's disappearance had broken her mother's heart as well as her own. Henry St. John had been branded a thief and a criminal, and her mother had been treated shabbily by her entire community—so badly, in fact, that the two of them had been forced to move to Clovis, New Mexico, to get away from the taunts and hateful behavior. Her mother, Theresa, had never truly recovered, and had also never remarried. She had loved Henry, still carried a torch for him in fact, and didn't accept that he had been guilty of the theft, despite the circumstantial evidence against him. Theresa was now fighting stage 4 pancreatic cancer and didn't have much time left on this earth. Luann was determined to find out the truth about her father, and hopefully prove his innocence, before her mother died.

Luann wasn't sure if she had the skills needed to discover the truth. She was an English professor at the local community college, not a trained investigator. But she had to try and give it her best, regardless. Her mother had always been her rock, and the one dependable person in her life. They enjoyed a wonderful relationship, and Luann wanted so much to give her this gift of knowledge about her father, before it was too late.

She shielded her eyes, said a short prayer of thanks that she had survived the crash with so little injury, and started climbing up the steep rocky slope. She wasn't sure she could make it, but she dug handholds and footholds out of the hard-packed earth the best she could and slowly headed up toward the road.

"Hello! Can I give you some help?"

She saw the proffered hand outstretched over the edge of the deep ditch just moments before she heard the words emanate from the kind masculine voice. A wave of relief swept over her, and even though she couldn't see the person attached to the hand, she reached out and took a hold of him with a firm grip. Just as her muscles had started to burn, help had arrived. God was indeed good—all the time. Despite these desperate circumstances, He had sent help.

"I'd sure appreciate that," she said thankfully.

His large brown fingers grasped her wrist tightly and lifted her out of the arroyo.

Joaquin Fuentes studied the woman carefully as he helped her back up to the road. He saw the blood on her face but didn't see any other visible injuries. He gave her a smile, hoping to ease the anxiety that he could see written across her features. She sure was a pretty woman, with dark brown curly hair pulled back with a headband and chocolate-colored eyes that were filled with relief and gratitude. "There we go, *señorita*. Now you're safe. Are you able to walk?"

She nodded but still gripped his hand. He could tell she was still shaken by the crash, and her arm trembled a bit as he supported her, despite her brave expression. "Why don't you come sit with me in my cruiser and enjoy the heat while I call for some help, okay? I think you're done driving for the day." He glanced back over the ledge of the arroyo at the smashed vehicle below. "I think your car might be done driving permanently."

He watched her closely as she glanced around and exhaled, apparently satisfied that they were alone and safe.

The sight of his law enforcement vehicle and uniform also seemed to help put her more at ease. She released his hand, then suddenly flinched at the sight of the large hairy dog that came ambling up beside him. Lobo was no small beast—he was well over a hundred pounds, and he looked more like a wild wolf than a pet. His fur was a mixture of gray, black and white, and the dark circles around his eyes made him look more ferocious than he actually was. It didn't help that he lowered his head and a deep guttural sound emanated from his throat. Joaquin recognized it as a friendly greeting, but the woman obviously wasn't sure what to make of that sound. She took a step backward and almost fell back into the arroyo.

Joaquin quickly reached out and took her arms, pulling her gently away from the precipice. "Whoa there, *señorita.* Lobo is harmless, unless you're a criminal, that is. He thinks he's a K-9 dog, despite his lack of certified police training. But I promise you, he won't hurt a lady like yourself."

"Is he a real wolf?" she asked, her tone shaky. Her eyes were still rounded and she raised an eyebrow.

Joaquin shook his head. "Nah. He just thinks he's a wolf. He's actually a long-haired Siberian husky. We use him to pull sleds in the snow during the winter." He reached over and used sign language to communicate that the dog should sit and stay. The dog obeyed instantly yet still issued a low whine. "He's a good boy, unless you have food around. Then you have to watch out. He always thinks he's starving. Mostly I just keep him around for the company. I do a lot of patrolling here in the mountains by myself. We get some tourists heading to Cedar Crest that run into trouble from time to time, but usually it's a quiet beat and I like having someone to talk to while I'm out here."

Luann glanced again at his cruiser that was parked off the road behind them. Then her gaze traveled over him, from his dark brown cowboy hat to his hiking boots, as if verifying that he was somebody she could trust. He liked her brown eyes. A man could get lost in eyes like that. And her skin was like porcelain, unblemished and fine. He wondered if her cheeks were as soft as they looked. She had a host of delicate features, including high cheekbones, a firm chin and Cupid's bow rosy lips. With each breath, warm moist air passed through those lips and created a small cloud of vapor. Joaquin mentally pinched himself. Good grief. He did not need to be noticing her lips or any other part of her. He was a law enforcement officer. He was here to do a job, nothing more. She was in trouble, and he was there to help.

"Are you the county sheriff?" she asked.

Thankfully, her words broke through his wayward thoughts. "I am," he said, nodding. "Joaquin Fuentes at your service."

She gave him a tentative smile. "My name is Luann. Luann St. John."

"Pleased to meet you. I don't recognize you as a local. Are you visiting from Albuquerque?"

"No," she replied. She didn't elaborate, so he continued.

"We get quite a few tourists each year that discover our little town and the surrounding area, but it looks like our roads were a bit treacherous for you. Maybe you took the curve a bit too fast? I'm glad I saw the smoke and dirt fly up from your accident. Otherwise, you might have been stuck for a while. I don't think there's much cell service out here." He paused and motioned toward the bend in the road. "We might need to ask the county to add some railing along this section. We sure don't want any other people getting hurt."

"I wasn't driving recklessly, I promise. There's something wrong with my car. The brakes wouldn't work properly. It's a rental, but it shouldn't have had a problem."

"Hmm. I'll have Gary at the shop check them out for you. He's the closest one with a wrecker back here. If your car has a mechanical problem, Gary can find it. He's a real pro. I'll give him a call in a minute, and we'll get you squared away. You'll probably need his report for the insurance, too."

He led her over to his car, opened the passenger door and pulled out the first-aid kit that he kept in the glove compartment. With a gentle hand, he found some gauze, added some witch hazel from a small bottle, and started dabbing at the blood over her eye. "You may need some stitches for this. I'll call you an ambulance."

"No thanks," she said, shaking her head. "I'm okay, and probably just need a butterfly bandage or some superglue to close up this wound." She stiffened her spine, and he admired her toughness and vibrancy that were quickly overcoming her shock. He noticed some scratches on her hands and cleaned them as well, then bandaged a couple of the larger scrapes. Her skin was soft, and her hands strong with neat, trim nails painted a metallic shade of blue.

"Well, ma'am, it's like this. You've been in a serious accident, and sometimes the injuries a person sustains aren't visible. We need to get you checked out by an expert, even if you don't think you need one. It's my duty to call. We do have an EMT based out of Tijeras, a town about twenty minutes away. He usually handles things like this whenever we need him." He finished cleansing the wound and handed her a sterile piece of gauze. "Here, the cut on your forehead has mostly stopped bleeding, and I think I got it clean, but let's put some pressure on it just in case while I call this in."

She took the pad and held it to her forehead while he reported the accident on his phone and requested the EMT and a wrecker to help retrieve her vehicle. He motioned for her to sit in the front passenger seat of his cruiser, closed the door behind her, and then circled the car and got in behind the wheel after letting Lobo into the back seat. Several times, he noticed her looking around the area, apparently making sure they were safe. Small worry lines had stretched across her forehead, and he noticed her fists clenching and unclenching. He wasn't sure, but it sure seemed like she was worried about more than just the fact that her rental car was at the bottom of an arroyo.

"Was there another car involved in your accident?" he asked gently.

"No, sir," she answered, shaking her head.

Joaquin frowned. "You keep glancing around the road. Are you expecting someone?"

She met his stare and her dark brown eyes locked with his own. When she spoke, her voice was deadly serious. "No. But I think someone just tried to kill me."

TWO

Joaquin leaned back, a surprised look on his face. "What? What do you mean?"

"I mean, this was no accident," Luann said firmly. "That car is a rental and is this year's model. It shouldn't be having any maintenance problems. I think someone tampered with my brakes. They were fine when I started out this morning, then they just quit working."

"Where are you coming from?"

"I went up to Fabio Rodriquez's house to talk. Do you know him?" When he nodded, she continued. "There's a car in his driveway, but even though I knocked, no one ever came to the door. I figured he didn't want to speak to me since I'm a stranger, so I turned around and came back. The brakes went out a few turns ago, and then I lost control of the car. I think someone doesn't want me here."

Joaquin tilted his head. "Whoa now, that's quite an accusation. Why were you trying to talk to Fabio?"

She paused. She could tell her words were bothering the sheriff, but who else should she tell? If a crime had been committed, he needed to know. "According to Susanna at the bed-and-breakfast where I'm staying, he's one of the older residents in Del Norte, and one of the few who was actually living in this area twenty years ago. I was hoping he could help me."

"Help you what?"

"Discover if my father was on that small plane that crashed back here in the mountains about twenty years ago."

Joaquin whistled. "There was a small plane that flew into the side of the mountain a while back. I was just a kid back then and lived down in Tijeras, but I've heard some stories—just rumors mostly. I really don't know much about it." He tilted his head. "What's your interest? Was your dad the pilot?"

"No, but I think he was forced on board by another man—someone who had just stolen some diamonds from the store where my father was working. I think the real thief wanted my father to take the blame, so he kidnapped him and then somehow escaped."

Joaquin frowned. "I don't remember any talk about diamonds. Are you sure we're talking about the same crash? From what I remember, there was only a pilot on board, and he was the only fatality. I certainly would have remembered if someone had found a cache of diamonds on the plane or somewhere near the crash site. That would have been all over the news—it's the stuff of legends. Hollywood might have even made a movie."

Was he teasing her? She wasn't sure and looked at him a little closer. He was a handsome man, with black hair cut in a military style, and smooth brown skin. He had dark brown eyes—almost black. The more she looked, the more she realized there wasn't laughter in those depths. His expression was one of genuine interest and thoughtful contemplation. He was really listening to her, not just humoring her as past law enforcement officers had done. His attention was actually refreshing, and she found herself warmed on the inside. Finally, Luann shrugged. "I'm not sure about all of the details. That's why I'm here—to find out what really happened. How many plane crashes do you get up here?"

"I'm not aware of any others, but you're right. If anyone would know and be able to help you learn more about what happened, it would be Fabio. He's lived here all his life and seems to know everyone. He's retired now, but he still comes down to the café in Del Norte sometimes to shoot the breeze. I see him around from time and time."

Luann was encouraged by his interest, so she pushed ahead. "I'm hoping maybe the thief and my dad might have escaped with parachutes right before the crash. It was a skydiving plane they were on, but I don't know for sure what happened, or what equipment was on board. According to the people I spoke to at the airport in Las Cruces where the plane took off from, there were usually two or more parachutes available. But the plane wasn't supposed to be used that day, so it might not have been loaded with any equipment." She drew her lips into a thin line. "Or maybe they both died and their bodies were just never found. There are a lot of unanswered questions about the whole affair. That's why I'm here. To see if I can find out anything at all about what really happened."

"Well, if they did survive, what happened to your dad?" He leaned forward. "He didn't come back to you?"

Luann cringed inwardly. That was the crux of the entire story. Had her dad survived but abandoned his family? Was he even now living it up on some exotic island, toasting his successful felony? Or was he a victim of the crime and never made it home because he died somewhere along the way—murdered by the thief who'd taken him hostage and forced him to be an accessory to the crime? Not knowing the truth ate her up inside. "He never came back," she admitted. "The authorities think that he and the other man disappeared with the diamonds and got away with the theft. They're not even sure my dad and the thief got on the plane. But my mom thinks he was forced to participate in that robbery. She's still holding out hope that, somehow, I'll find something that proves his innocence."

"Does she think he's dead?"

Luann took a deep breath, the pain still tightening her heart. "I think it's easier for her to believe that he died rather than that he abandoned us. I know she still loves him and won't hear a word against him. She's convinced he was a victim."

Joaquin nodded. "I get that. It sounds like true love. I'm impressed by her devotion." He paused and tilted his head. "This sounds almost like a plot from a romance novel." He furrowed his brow. "What do you think?"

Luann smiled brightly, trying to push away the melancholy that had suddenly swept over her. Those feelings of abandonment just wouldn't dissipate, no matter what she did. She was afraid to get close—afraid to really get to know anyone— because she didn't want to face the pain of losing the relationship later on. That's why her one and only boyfriend had given up on her a year or so ago. It was easier—safer—to just do things on her own without depending on anybody else. But loneliness was an entirely different difficulty. She sighed, trying to seal her feelings inside. "I think I'd like to know the truth—one way or another. That's why I'm here."

Joaquin quirked an eyebrow. Was it pain causing the shadow in her eyes? And why not? He himself had been abandoned about two years ago by the woman who had vowed to love him forever. His wife had shredded his heart when she'd left, and it had scarred him so badly that he had given up romantic relationships for the rest of his life. He hadn't dated since. He knew all about heart-wrenching pain. He studied Luann's hands that still clenched and unclenched. She probably didn't even realize she was doing it, but her body language and facial expression were fierce. She definitely believed in her quest and was quite committed to her cause. An urge to help her suddenly swept over him, which was a surprise. Assisting her with her queries went beyond his normal job duties, but there was something about this woman—something that drew him in and made him want to protect her and help her discover the facts that might actually give her some resolution and peace. His mind sifted through the details she'd described. "So, you're saying Fabio wasn't able to help?"

Luann shrugged. "He wouldn't even come to the door. That's the same response I've gotten from everyone here so far that I've approached. Either they don't know, or they don't want to talk about it. Some people have even been openly hostile. This conversation I'm having with you right now is the longest one I've had since I arrived in Del Norte." She brushed a stray curl out of her eyes. "I guess I understand. This is a small town, and I'm an outsider. Add to that that I'm asking about something that happened twenty years ago. I guess it's no wonder folks are wary and don't have much to say."

Joaquin made a quick decision. He was just a small county sheriff, but he did have the local connections needed to assist her. He'd been in Del Norte and the surrounding area most of his life and knew virtually everyone who inhabited these parts. "I'm going to help you. As soon as our EMT gives you the okay, and Gary gets here to get your car out of the arroyo, we'll head back up to Fabio's, and I'll see if I can convince him to talk to you."

Luann smiled and Joaquin couldn't help but notice how that simple expression lit up her entire face. Even her body language changed, and she had a hopeful stance. Her happiness made him feel warm inside despite the chilly air.

No. He was not attracted to her. He was just helping out a struggling citizen in his jurisdiction. He was being kind to a tourist. That was part of his job, wasn't it?

Before she could respond, or he could wrestle with his feelings any further, he saw the ambulance pull up behind his car. He motioned for her to follow him and walked Luann over to the EMT. A few minutes after she'd had the wound treated over her eyebrow and completed her brief exam, Gary also arrived on the scene with his wrecker and started the job of retrieving Luann's car from the arroyo. Before Gary was too involved, Joaquin pulled him aside.

"The lady says she had some trouble with her brakes. Can you check them out for me and let me know what you find?"

"Sure thing, Sheriff," Gary agreed. "Happy to help."

A short time later, Joaquin and Luann stood on Fabio's doorstep while Lobo sniffed the ground nearby where some prickly pear cactus was growing. Fabio's house was more of a cabin, and the rustic wooden building was small but well kept. As far as Joaquin knew, Fabio had never been married, and the older man preferred the quiet and solitary life of being out in the woods to the hustle and bustle found over in Albuquerque, the large city on the other side of the mountain. Fabio was retired now and lived off some sort of government pension. Joaquin wasn't quite sure what the man had done in his younger days and made a mental note to find out more about him just to satisfy his own curiosity.

Lobo suddenly surprised him by giving a low whimper, and the dog startled when Joaquin shifted, as if he were tense or afraid. Joaquin reached down and rubbed him affectionately behind the ears, but the dog stayed on alert, his eyes scanning the area. "Easy there, boy. Everything okay?" Joaquin knocked again but still got no response.

"Does Fabio have another vehicle?" Luann asked as she motioned to the four-door sedan that was parked in the driveway in front of the cruiser.

"Not that I know of. That's his car. I've seen him driving it. He should be here." Joaquin took a few steps and tried to peer in the front window, but the curtains blocked his view. He returned to the front door and tried the knob. It turned easily in his hand.

"Fabio? It's Sheriff Fuentes. Are you okay?" He called out as he pushed the door open and stepped inside. "Fabio?"

There was still no answer, and a few seconds later, Joaquin knew why.

Fabio Rodriquez lay prone on his living room floor, a pool of blood circling his midriff.

Joaquin rushed over to Fabio's side and felt for a pulse.

Nothing. The man was lying on his back, his eyes still staring sightlessly at the ceiling with a surprised expression on his face. Several stab wounds were visible across his chest, and a thin trail of blood had seeped from his mouth and collected under his shoulder with the blood from his torso. His lips were a whitish blue, and his dark brown skin had an ashen cast that made him look sickly.

Joaquin glanced up and saw Luann reach down and take a hold of Lobo's collar. They had come in behind him and were standing on the threshold. She'd closed the door behind them, probably to keep out the cold. Her skin had visibly paled, and a look of disbelief and worry painted her features as she looked at Fabio's body. "Is he dead?"

"Yes. He's been murdered."

She gasped and covered her mouth with her free hand. "How long ago?"

"At least seven to eight hours would be my guess. Maybe a little less. We don't get this kind of crime up here, so I'll have to call in the experts." He stood and pulled out his phone, reporting the scene and, for the second time today, asking for assistance. Thankfully, the EMT who had helped Luann after the car accident was still nearby, and would also be the one to come and retrieve Fabio's body after the scene was investigated. They'd have to wait a bit longer though for a trained homicide detective to arrive from Albuquerque, but that couldn't be helped. Murder was a far cry from the types of crimes Joaquin usually investigated, and he wasn't too proud to admit that he needed some assistance. Thankfully, he had a friend in the New Mexico State Police Investigations Bureau who had a bigger budget and a willing ear. He finished his calls and stowed his phone, then turned back to Luann. "If you don't mind, please stay right there by the door and keep holding Lobo like you're doing. I need to preserve the crime scene, but I'd also like to take a look around to see if I can figure out what happened here."

"Of course," she agreed.

Lobo growled and his ears pricked up again, but Joaquin still heard nothing. He wasn't sure what was going on here, but his own senses were on high alert, just like the dog's. Who would want to hurt Fabio? He was just a harmless retired state employee who liked drinking black coffee, talking about politics at the café and deer hunting with a muzzleloader. He'd always been friendly and, as far as Joaquin knew, didn't have any enemies. He glanced back over at Luann but couldn't imagine that Fabio's murder and Luann's quest had anything in common. After all, the plane crash that claimed Luann's focus had occurred over twenty years ago. Fabio had been murdered today.

He turned his attention back to the scene.

The cabin was basically set up like a studio apartment, with the kitchen and living room on one side, and a bed and storage area on the other. Through a door to the side, Joaquin could make out a full bath with a linen closet. Next to the single bed there was a large desk covered with books and loose papers. Joaquin pulled out a pair of rubber gloves, instantly thankful for his practice of always keeping a pair in his pocket. He snapped them on, then approached the desk and took a look at the various papers. One stack was of old bills that were marked

"Paid," and another was correspondence with the City of Albuquerque regarding some old traffic tickets. He looked up at the pegboard that covered the wall over the desk and was surprised to see a large map of the area that was separated into grids. Each square seemed to represent a five-mile section. Most of the grid squares were marked through with a large red X, but three of the squares over a rocky area of land with a deep ravine running through it were still open and had no markings at all.

Joaquin leaned forward to take a better look. He'd backpacked out on the mountainside as a teenager with his Boy Scout troop, but didn't recognize the ravine. It looked like it was in an area that would actually be pretty hard to access, at least with a vehicle. Horses would probably be required.

What was Fabio doing?

Joaquin pulled out his phone again and snapped a picture of the map. He wasn't sure what it signified, if anything, but it certainly wasn't something he'd ever come across before. He glanced at the books and moved them slightly so he could read the titles. They were a collection of various tomes about the area. Some covered the history of Tijeras, the nearby larger town, while others described forensic investigations and true crime stories. A few boasted titles about precious metals and gemstones.

Gemstones? Joaquin glanced around again, looking for a rock tumbler or other paraphernalia that most of the local artisans used to make jewelry, but didn't see any of the telltale signs. Had Fabio decided to try his hand at making and selling necklaces and whatnot like many of the other locals did?

Suddenly, the glass in the front window by the couch

shattered, followed by a cold swoosh of air that touched him even as far away as where he was standing by the desk. A few seconds later, a Molotov cocktail hit the floor and fire instantly spread across the rug. A second incendiary bomb broke through the small pane of glass in the second window, and Luann shrieked and pulled Lobo aside just as the surrounding curtains and wall went up in flames. The dog started barking, pulling against his collar, but Luann held fast, keeping him away from the fire. The air filled with the acrid scent of burning gasoline, and black smoke started to rise and fill the small room. The flames spread quickly, a lake of yellow edged in blue.

They had to get out now. The fire was already absorbing most of the oxygen in the room, and the heat was intense.

If they didn't move quickly, they were as good as dead.

THREE

Luann could barely breathe.

The black smoke burned her eyes and throat even as she spun around and tried to open the front door. Her chest felt tight, and her fingers were shaking so badly it was hard to make them work properly. She swallowed hard and twisted against the knob, but the front door wouldn't budge. A surge of adrenaline swept over her as the fear started to grow. She quickly examined the dead bolt, but it held fast, and she couldn't get the lever to turn to disengage the lock. No matter what she did, neither the bolt nor the door would open. Luann didn't know how, but somebody must have locked or barred the door from the outside after they'd all entered the cabin. There was a small peephole in the center of the door, but no other opening. She looked outside and saw a silver truck disappearing down the drive, a plume of smoke following behind it. She couldn't see the driver, or even any of the numbers on the yellow New Mexican license plate, but the driver had to be the one who'd done this. Anyone else would have stayed to help.

Who wanted her dead? Who had killed Fabio?

It didn't matter. Right now, the only thing that was important was escaping this building before it became an inferno. She glanced around the small cabin, but the only windows were already blocked off by the fire. Flames were licking up the wall hangings and the surrounding walls, blistering the chemicals in the wood. How were they going to escape? She kept a firm grip on Lobo and turned frantically to Joaquin as he appeared by her side. He had removed his gloves and had a grim expression on his face.

"The front door won't budge. I can't open it," she yelled. A bout of coughing overtook her and she felt Joaquin's hand on her back in a gentle touch of reassurance as he helped her bend toward the floor where there was a little less smoke. She barely knew this man, but his calm acceptance of their deadly situation helped ease the panic that had formed a hard knot in her stomach and was causing adrenaline to spurt into her joints. He nodded his acknowledgment of her words, and once the coughing ended, he motioned for her to move closer to Lobo and handed her a red bandana.

"Here, put this over your mouth and nose," he said as he pulled his shirt up over his own mouth. He motioned with his head once she had followed his directions. "Let's try the back. I'll get Lobo. Follow right behind me, okay?" She nodded and felt his hand replace hers on Lobo's collar so she had her hands free. Then, in a low crouch, he started leading them toward the back door by following the wall. The cabin was small, and already mostly engulfed in the flames that were lapping at the ceiling and the floor everywhere the gasoline had touched. The pungent smell of burning fuel and plastic mixed with the chemicals in the treated wood of the floor and walls, and her eyes continued to burn as they made the trek to the back door. Heat from the fire radiated against her skin, and she felt beads of sweat pop out against her brow and down her back.

Even as they crawled, they both coughed and struggled to see through the thick black smoke. Lobo sensed their distress and started whining and barking as he scrunched closer to the ground.

Luann heard Joaquin say something to the dog near his ear, and the dog instantly quieted. A few seconds later, they reached the back door, and Luann felt Joaquin reach for her hand and put it on Lobo's collar again. "Keep your head down, and hold him for me, okay? I'm going to see if I can get us out of here."

Luann nodded. His face was mere inches away, and she was close enough to glimpse the determination in Joaquin's eyes, even as the smoke swirled between them. A small part of her was afraid that he would leave her, yet the fear she was feeling warred against the fact that he was still right beside her, working to save them both. He was the sheriff. He had a duty to protect and serve, right? But even if he didn't, she knew instinctively that this man was not going to abandon her. There was something about him—something that testified to his decency and dedication to helping others.

She started coughing again and he reached over and squeezed her hand, then quickly released it. The touch bolstered her courage and reassured her. She wasn't alone. He was going to help. She knew instinctively by that simple act that he wouldn't abandon her.

"Move back a bit," he said as he motioned with his hands. He waited a few seconds until she had settled against the wall, then reached for the back doorknob. She watched him verify that the lock was disengaged, but no matter what he did to try to open it, the door still wouldn't budge. He pushed aside the curtain and checked the top part of the door and Luann got a glimpse of the nine rectangular panels of glass that made up the upper section. Joaquin disappeared into the smoke for a moment, then returned with a wooden chair in his hands. With a shout, he slammed it against the door, breaking the glass and the thin wooden frames that held the panels in place. The chair broke, too, and pieces of wood and glass scattered around the floor. Air rushed into the room, and the extra oxygen made the flames in the cabin suddenly surge. Even so, the new air was welcome, and some of the heavy smoke poured through the opening. A few seconds later, the air was slightly easier to breathe.

Lobo whimpered, and she rubbed his head with her free hand as Joaquin used a piece of wood from the broken chair to clear out the rest of the glass from the edges of the frame. As she watched, he reached through the opening, trying to discover what was holding the door closed, yet no matter what he tried to remove the barrier, the door still held fast.

Another wave of fear gripped her. If the door wouldn't open, were they going to be able to get through the top panel of the door where the glass had been? She didn't see any other option. Joaquin continued to work at the door, and even though she couldn't see everything that he was trying, she could hear him kicking and wrestling against the wood. The flames were mere seconds away from overcoming the entire building now and her skin was hot and sweaty and felt scorched and tight. They had to get out—immediately. Their very lives depended upon what Joaquin did in the next few minutes.

Joaquin's lungs felt like they were being scoured with sandpaper, every breath dragging fire into his chest. Smoke thickened the air until it blurred the walls and floor into a shifting haze, but even through the choking fog, his gaze found her.

Luann.

His red bandana was tied snugly across her nose and mouth, and her hair was plastered against her temples, damp with sweat. She clutched Lobo tightly, arms trembling, but her eyes—dark, clear, steady—were fixed on him. Even in the middle of an inferno, she wasn't crumbling. That quiet strength bolstered his own resolve. They weren't going to die here. He refused to let that happen.

The back door mocked him, sealing the small cabin like a tomb. The dead bolt had been bent or tampered with, wedged in such a way that it wouldn't open. Outside, heavy logs had been stacked across the porch, a barricade that made escape nearly impossible. The wood had been placed there deliberately. Someone had trapped them inside.

A fresh surge of heat pressed against his back, and with it came a realization that clawed at his gut—this wasn't just an attack. It was a message. Whoever had set this blaze wanted Luann silenced and her quest to disappear.

And him with her.

Who in Del Norte would murder three people?

The fire cracked like gunshots, and the flames leaped from the floorboards and licked greedily at the walls. Smoke clawed at his throat until he doubled over coughing, but when he raised his head, she was still there, holding on to Lobo, her gaze searching for his. That single look once again steadied him in a way that nothing else could.

He had been sheriff of Del Norte for a few years, but this—murder, arson, attempted execution—was beyond anything his quiet county usually saw. His job was ticketing careless drivers and breaking up bar fights, not facing death in a burning cabin. He'd never worked a homicide even once in his career, never chased a killer. But none of that mattered now. He had one job tonight: protect Luann, no matter the cost. He would have to figure out the "why" behind Fabio's murder and the arson later, once they were safe. Right now, he had to focus on escape and nothing else.

A thunderous groan split the rafters and a burning beam fell with a violent crash, spewing sparks across the floor. Instinct drove him forward. He shoved her flat against the wall, his arms braced on either side of her as the fire flared in front of them. The heat licked across his back, singeing his coat, but he barely felt it. What he did feel was her grip, tight around his sleeve, holding on as though she drew strength from him. The contact jolted through him—hotter than the flames, more dangerous than the smoke. He'd had a beautiful woman in his life before, and she had abandoned him, leaving his heart torn in shreds. He never would again. So why was this woman affecting him so? That thought also had to be saved for later. Right now, he had to focus on escape and escape alone.

"Window," he rasped, his voice shredded raw.

She blinked, coughed, then looked up at him with eyes

that shimmered even in the choking haze. For a moment, it was as though they were suspended outside the chaos—the fire roaring, the roof moaning overhead, yet the only thing that existed was the line tethering her gaze to his.

Her lips moved beneath the soot-stained bandana. "What about you?"

Joaquin leaned closer, so close that the smoke blurred and all he saw was her—her damp lashes, the faint tremor of her breath. "You first," he said. "Then Lobo, then me. We'll be right behind you. I promise."

Something flickered in her expression, something that wasn't fear so much as belief. She nodded once, firm. Her expression hit him like a load of bricks.

Trust. She trusted him. But how could she? They barely knew each other. Still, the confidence was there in her eyes, reflected back at him so strongly that it stiffened his determination and made his muscles bunch, ready to push forward.

He slid his arms around her, lifting her off the ground. Her body pressed against his chest—warm, tense, alive—and for a brief, stolen second, he felt the steady beat of her heart against his ribs. His muscles screamed from the effort, but he didn't let her go until he'd guided her legs through the jagged glass. The shards scraped her jeans as sparks rained down from above, but she never faltered.

His hands lingered at her waist longer than they should have, unwilling to release her into the night, but then she slipped through. She disappeared into the smoke outside, and his chest ached at the loss.

A dog's insistent bark broke through his haze. Lobo was still trapped with him. Joaquin stumbled to the husky, gathering the trembling weight into his arms. The dog's nails scrabbled against his chest as he shoved him through the window. On the other side, Luann's voice called softly, urging, coaxing. He caught a glimpse of her through the smoke, hands outstretched, steadying Lobo. Relief washed through him. She was there. She was safe. And so was his dog. They were both going to survive.

Now him.

Joaquin braced his blistered palms on the searing frame, the heat biting into his skin. His body sagged, starved for oxygen, vision swimming in shades of gray and black. He wanted to drop. To give in. But then he thought of her—the way she'd looked at him before she crawled out, the weight of her trust. She was waiting for him. Depending on him.

That thought alone gave him the strength to push. He hauled himself upward, dragging his legs over the threshold, scraping across the splintered wood until his boots found purchase on the pile outside.

The cabin behind him gave a final, violent roar. The roof collapsed inward, the sound deafening as fire swallowed the place whole. Sparks burst into the night, raining down like molten stars.

He staggered free, collapsing onto the ground, coughing so hard his ribs ached. His chest hurt, along with his hands. Another loud bang sounded behind him, and he turned to watch the cabin fall in on itself until it was reduced to nothing but ash and flame.

Whoever had tried to take Luann's life tonight had made the worst mistake of their life, because he wasn't going to stop until they were prosecuted to the fullest extent of the law.

FOUR

A wave of panic swept through Luann as she saw the building collapse. The fire spit sparks and flames into the air as the framing and roof crumpled. and the heat and the acrid smell intensified substantially. She held Lobo's collar tightly as her eyes scanned through the billowing smoke and piles of debris, searching frantically for Joaquin. She barely registered the ambulance that pulled into the yard and parked a few feet away from her and only gave the EMT a cursory nod as the fear swelled in her chest. Had Joaquin survived?

"The sheriff!" she shouted over the roar of the fire. "He was right behind me!"

"Okay, we'll find him!" the tech yelled as he shielded his eyes and and joined in her search.

Was Joaquin alive? Nothing else mattered. The man had saved her life. She had to find out whether or not he had gotten out of the cabin and survived. The two continued the search through the churning smoke until they finally saw Joaquin, lying prone on the ground, coughing. Relief made her knees weak as they both rushed to his side. Joaquin had his arm across his forehead and his clothes were dirty and singed, but he noticed them approach and acknowledged them with a small hand gesture as he struggled to breathe. Lobo broke free from Luann's grip and surged towards his master, barking and pawing at the ground. Joaquin reached out and gave him a reassuring pat, just as another bout of coughing overtook him.

"Help me get him to the ambulance," the EMT said loudly over the roar of the inferno.

Luann nodded her agreement and they both bent and grabbed Joaquin under one of his arms near the shoulder and carefully helped him stand and move toward the rig. The heat was blistering, and she could still smell the intense stench of burning chemicals, wood and plastics. Lobo followed close by, alternating between barking and whining. He was clearly in distress because his owner was hurt, and he wasn't quite sure what to do about it.

Luann glanced at the EMT and said a quick prayer of thanks. She recognized the red-haired man as the same one who had helped her just a short time ago by the roadside after her car accident, and she was glad he'd still been relatively close and had arrived so quickly on the scene. Joaquin was a large man, and she doubted she could have managed to move him away from the fire by herself. She gave him a smile, noticing for the first time that his name, "Dan", was embroidered on his shirt. The two of them slowly lead Joaquin over to the back bumper of the emergency vehicle and helped him sit.

A few seconds later, Dan had secured oxygen masks for both of them, gotten Joaquin situated on a stretcher, and was checking the sheriff's vitals. Luann noticed a folded body bag in one of the labeled compartments, and realized the EMT would also have the sad duty of retrieving Fabio's body once the fire was extinguished.

She studied Dan carefully as she took several deep breaths of the wonderfully clean air flowing through the mask. He was probably in his thirties, with a receding hairline and strong facial features that made him seem intense yet approachable. His motions were efficient and professional as he worked, yet there was also a deep concern in his eyes that he couldn't quite mask. It was obvious from both men's behavior that they not only knew each other, but were good friends. In fact, based on their body language and verbal sparring that each man had been muttering under their breath, Luann wouldn't have been surprised if they'd known each other their entire lives. When Joaquin tried to rise from the stretcher, Dan's voice hardened and he talked to Joaquin in a voice that only a friend could probably get away with. "You're laying right there until you can breathe normally, and I finish checking you over for burns. Do you understand?"

"I hear you," Joaquin said through the mask. "The whole county can hear you. But that doesn't mean I have to like it."

"I didn't say you had to like it," Dan said with a tinge of sarcasm and a wink. "But I'm in charge until I clear you, and you'll do what I say until that actually happens. Got it?"

The testosterone was so thick in the air Luann could almost see it. She grinned, unable to stop herself from reacting to their playful banter. Somehow, their behavior began to ease the tension that was still tightening the muscles across her chest. Joaquin and she had survived this latest threat, and both of them were going to be okay.

Carefully, the EMT used his scissors to start removing the damaged sleeves of Joaquin's coat. "Let's see what's under here," he said as he cut away the burned fabric. Joaquin coughed, and Dan turned and fiddled with the dial on the oxygen tank, then finished with the ruined coat, carefully moving the singed shirt sleeves out of the way as well as he started examining the sheriff's burns. Thankfully, the majority of the damage was on his hands, and hadn't spread up his arms. Joaquin was covered with dirt and soot, and the hair on his head was even a tad singed, but overall, the look on Dan's face told Luann that Joaquin's burns were minor. The tech worked quickly, inspecting his friend's injuries, all the while keeping an eye on Joaquin's improving oxygen levels.

Joaquin closed his eyes and took deep breaths, finally submitting to the other man's assistance.

Dan noticed Luann shiver and motioned for her to get into the back of the rig as well. She complied and leaned back in the chair provided, relief flowing through her veins. They were safe, for now. But who had killed Fabio, and who had tried to kill them as well? Did the murder have anything to do with her, or was it a totally separate incident? She was mentally exhausted, and nothing seemed to make sense.

Suddenly, distant sirens broke into her thoughts, announcing that the fire department and others were on their way. She glanced at the cabin that was totally engulfed in flames and blew out a breath as she watched two squad cars and a firetruck pull into the front yard. The cabin was a complete loss, but hopefully the firefighters could keep the fire from spreading into the surrounding forest.

Firemen jumped down from the rig and immediately started fitting hoses to the tank on the back of the truck, while the law enforcement officers circled the building, apparently assessing the damage and the safety risks. One seemed to be a sheriff's deputy and wore a uniform similar to what Joaquin was wearing, while the other was taller and was dressed in clothing that identified him as a state trooper. Luann didn't know how law enforcement agencies worked and cooperated with each other but imagined that anyone nearby would come and help when they heard the call.

Joaquin continued to allow Dan to doctor his wounds, but he suddenly reached over and gently nudged Luann. She turned her head and their eyes met. "Are you okay?" he asked through the plastic mask.

Dan was busy with his bandages, but he glanced up at Luann as well, apparently also wanting an answer.

"I am, thanks to you. You saved my life." She patted his shoulder, unable to keep from reaching out. "Thank you." She started coughing, and the EMT shook his head and turned her oxygen up a notch.

About fifteen minutes later, Dan had finished his exams of both of his patients, and had almost finished dealing with the burns on Joaquin's hands. Luann took off her mask, declared herself quite restored, and jumped down from the truck, leaving Dan to work on his more severely injured patient.

A third law enforcement vehicle arrived on the scene, and Luann reached out and grabbed Lobo's collar so he stayed out of the way as the firemen worked. Although Fabio's cabin was somewhat remote, nearby neighbors also started to arrive and block the driveway, and the law enforcement officers had cordoned off the area and were now talking in a small group, keeping an eye on the bystanders as well as the firemen who continued to battle the blaze.

A moment later, Joaquin hopped down from the ambulance wearing a new blue T-shirt. Both of his hands were loosely bandaged with a clean, sterile wrap up to his wrists, and he had on some sort of oversized gloves that added another layer of protection to his damaged skin. He'd been wearing a coat before, but probably didn't need one now since the fire was still giving off an intense heat throughout the surrounding area. He greeted Lobo, then sat down beside Luann on the bumper and met her eyes. There was kindness there, as well as pain that he was trying to disguise. His burns were probably really hurting, but the smile he gave her was concerned and friendly. "I'll find you a ride back to town as soon as I can," he said regretfully. "I'm going to be here awhile and don't want you to have to stick around unnecessarily."

"I'd rather wait for you, actually," Luann said, with a motion to Lobo. "I can keep an eye on your dog while you work."

"Are you sure you don't mind?" he asked, his eyebrow raised.

"Positive," Luann replied. Someone had tried to kill her twice today and had succeeded at killing Fabio. She wasn't anxious to go back to civilization where she didn't know who to trust and who the murderer might be. She started coughing and Joaquin touched her gently on her shoulder. "Okay, but like I said, it's going to be a while. If you change your mind, just get my attention and let me know. Your car is probably at the repair shop by now, but odds are you're going to just need a new rental. Maybe you can call and get that taken care of while I'm working. Do you have your cell phone?"

"Yes. Good idea. Hopefully, they'll deliver." Her purse was still slung across her chest, and thankfully, she still had her phone and her wallet.

Joaquin shrugged. "If they don't, I'll drive you over to Albuquerque tomorrow and we'll get you squared away." He turned his attention to Lobo and gave him a hand signal. "Lobo, stay with Luann."

The dog barked in response, and Luann was impressed that the gloves didn't hinder their communication. She liked dogs but had never owned one. Were they all this smart? She wasn't sure, but Lobo seemed to be in a class by himself.

As Luann watched, Joaquin walked over to other law enforcement officers who were standing out of the firemen's way but still keeping an eye on the gathering crowd. They talked for quite a while, and she imagined he was reporting what had happened to Fabio and everything that had transpired afterward. Her eyes turned to the firemen who were spraying water on the fire and making progress at dousing the conflagration. There was no way the cabin or anything in it was salvageable, but they seemed to be doing a good job of keeping the flames from spreading into the surrounding woods. New Mexico was a dry state, with very little humidity and few water sources. The entire mountainside could be easily ravaged by a forest fire if one got out of control.

Eventually, Joaquin made his way over to the crowd standing behind the police tape. It was easy to see that he knew most if not all of them, and he spoke to each one, greeting them and smiling, despite stopping a few times due to coughing. His position was probably elected, so it made sense that he would reach out, especially during scary situations. But even so, Joaquin's actions didn't seem practiced or forced. In fact, he seemed to genuinely care about each of the people he was speaking to. Still, Luann couldn't help but wonder. Was someone in the gathering crowd a murderer? She'd seen stories on TV where an arsonist had come back to watch the destruction he'd caused. And didn't murderers sometimes return to the scene of the crime as well? She studied the faces of the onlookers but had no idea if the guilty party was one of the crowd or not. Had whoever killed Fabio come back to finish the job by burning the evidence? Was the murderer one of Joaquin's neighbors and friends? A sliver of fear swept up her spine as she continued to study the faces of the people. Was the killer watching her even now?

Suddenly, Luann realized that one of the men near the edge of the crowd was glaring at her. He was tall and lanky with bushy brown hair and a scruffy beard and appeared to be in his early twenties or so. She couldn't remember his name but recognized him as someone she'd seen at the diner before—he'd been picking up food while she'd been eating at one of the booths. His expression was openly hostile, and his eyes burned into her. Then, before she could even think of what to do about his behavior, he turned and disappeared into the crowd.

Why would he glare at her? She didn't know his name or anything about him, and he'd probably only been a small child when her father disappeared. Why would he care that she was here in Del Norte, asking questions? Why did he hate her when he didn't even know her? His actions were more than just odd—they were unsettling and scary, especially after everything she had experienced today.

Was the skinny, scruffy man the one who had tried to kill her?

A few hours later, Joaquin was finally ready to leave what was left of Fabio's cabin. The fire had been doused, and thankfully had been stopped before it had spread into the tree line. Once the fire had cooled somewhat and the fire marshal had declared it safe, the entire scene had been photographed, and then Dan and another officer had retrieved Fabio's remains, zipped up the body bag, and headed to the morgue over in Albuquerque. Most of the onlookers had also disappeared, with only a handful still standing behind the yellow crime scene tape. Joaquin knew those who remained and had a hard time imagining that any of the locals were capable of murder. Still, he had surreptitiously asked the photographer to take photos of the crowd, just in case he needed to revisit the identities of the onlookers at any point in the investigation.

He put his hands on his hips and surveyed the crime scene one final time. The cabin was completely destroyed, and nothing recognizable remained besides the old iron bathtub, some scorched pots and pans and some horseshoes that Fabio had used as decorations in his living room. From his initial assessment and observations, the fire marshal had stated the accelerant was most likely gasoline, but he promised to have the lab run a few tests to confirm his findings once he returned to his office. Unfortunately, they hadn't discovered anything that pointed toward anyone in particular as the murderer. There were no known arsonists operating in the area, and no obvious evidence that pointed to a particular person. Joaquin was thankful he'd had the presence of mind to photograph the map and the inside of the cabin before the fire had destroyed it all. He didn't know what any of the clues meant yet, and he had his work cut out for him.

The air was turning chilly now that the fire was out, and he shivered involuntarily. Thankfully, the wind had died down. His arms were hurting from the burns, but he was glad his hands had been spared for the most part, and the gloves were helping. He realized that, overall, he'd been incredibly blessed not to have sustained even more serious injuries. He said a silent prayer of thanks, then turned toward Luann who had moved at some point and was now sitting on a fallen log near his cruiser. Lobo lay at her feet, keeping a watchful eye on both her and Joaquin, and he was glad his dog was there, keeping her company.

He'd never met Luann before today, yet they had already been through so much together, and he felt a protectiveness surge within him whenever she was near. The feelings surprised him. He'd been married before and, unbidden, the image of Harper flashed in his mind's eye: Harper smiling at him on their wedding day. Harper yelling at *him* in anger when he'd caught her cheating on him, as if her actions had somehow been his fault instead of hers. Harper lying to him as she drove off, abandoning both him and their young daughter, never to be heard from again except for when he'd gotten the divorce papers in the mail.

He pushed the thoughts of Harper aside. He was tired, dirty and hurting. The last thing he wanted to do right now was add his emotional scars to the mix and relive the painful memories. He approached Luann, who greeted him with a smile. "Ready to go?" he asked.

"Sure thing," she agreed as she stood and brushed off her pants. "I think I'm going to avoid campfires for the foreseeable future, even if they do have s'mores available."

"Me, too," Joaquin quipped with a smile. He was glad she was able to find some humor in what had otherwise been a terrifying day. He led her to his car and soon, with Lobo in the back seat, they were headed back toward Del Norte. His hands were sore, but he was able to drive, and once again, he found himself praying with thankfulness. The day could have turned out infinitely worse. God had definitely been looking out for them.

Although Joaquin was physically spent, he couldn't stop his mind from wandering. Why had someone tried to kill them? What clues had been destroyed in the fire? He glanced sideways at Luann. He didn't have any proof, but his gut was telling him that everything that had transpired today had something to do with his passenger and her quest to uncover the past. But what was the connection?

"So, can you tell me more about your father's disappearance?" Joaquin asked gently.

Luann shrugged. "Well, I had a friend who worked at the local police department who helped me get copies of the police reports and the surveillance videos, so I know a little about what happened. My dad's name was Henry St. John. From what the few witnesses reported, he went to work like it was any other day. He was the manager of the local jewelry store, and there is footage of him opening the store at 8:00 a.m. like he did every morning."

"And nothing looked amiss?"

"Nothing. He was even whistling as he unlocked the front door and flipped the sign to Open. He waited on a few customers, and around 11:30, an unknown stranger entered the store, and he took him into the back storage room. The camera never got a clear visual of the visitor's face, and he was never identified. All the police could tell was that he seemed to be in his early thirties and was of average build. He was wearing a large-brimmed cowboy hat and a suit. Then, my dad and that unknown man left the store. My dad put the Closed sign up on his way out and locked the front door behind him, and then the two men walked out of camera range. The store never reopened after lunch, and when the owner arrived later that afternoon, he discovered that almost two million dollars in diamonds was missing."

"Was your dad ever seen again?"

"The police say no. But later that day, a local skydiving plane was stolen from the general aviation tarmac. A grainy video from the flight line security tape seemed to show my dad and two other men near the stolen plane. One was wearing a baseball cap, and his face was also never captured. The other was a known pilot who died in that crash you heard about when you were a kid. The problem was nobody saw my dad or the other man get on the plane. The camera angle wasn't good, and the footage was poor, even after it was enhanced. The pilot's remains were identified through DNA, but no other bodies were discovered near the crash site. The video was dismissed by local authorities, though, because the third man's face was also obscured, and the film was so rough, it was hard to even tell if the man was wearing the same clothes my dad was wearing when he disappeared. The police concluded that my dad stole the diamonds and disappeared with the man they saw with him at the store. They don't know if that was them at the airport, if they escaped by another plane or left town a totally different way. Eventually, the case went cold, and as far as I know, nobody has discovered any new evidence since. For all intents and purposes, my dad just disappeared that day."

Joaquin considered her words and mulled them over in his mind. "And what do you believe?"

Luann sighed and fisted her hands. "I want to believe that the airport footage shows that my dad was forced onto the plane and kidnapped, and that he did not willingly participate in the theft. I want to believe that, somehow, he got off that plane and survived, but in my gut, I think he's dead. He has to be. I think that if he really was alive, he would have come back to us, somehow, or at least somehow communicated with my mom. She and Dad loved each other. I can't believe he willingly abandoned her, or me. And I know in my heart he wasn't a criminal." She pushed a stray curl behind her ear. "But the cops think I'm wrong, and incredibly naive. They're convinced he was a thief, and that he and the unknown man pulled off the heist and disappeared together."

Joaquin pondered her words. It must be difficult to live without knowing what really happened that day. "Do you have a copy of the videos with you here in Del Norte?" he asked.

"I do," she replied.

Before the incident at Fabio's cabin, he might not have asked, but his gut was telling him that somehow the fire was related to Luann's quest. Someone had just tried to kill them both, and he was determined to find out who. His exhaustion seemed to disappear as he got his second wind.

"Let's go watch those recordings."

FIVE

Joaquin watched his passenger out of the corner of his eye. He knew she was anxious to share the video with him. From the way she talked, he seemed like the first person besides her mother who had really showed any sincere interest in her case in years. It had to be frustrating to be searching for answers without getting much support, and she almost seemed to be grasping at straws, going down any rabbit trail that might reveal the truth. Could her father have even boarded that plane that crashed here so many years ago? There was no proof.

He shrugged to himself as he considered the possibilities. He was curious to see the videos himself. The cold case had grabbed his interest, if for no other reason than because Luann was so passionate in her quest. Still, by the time they reached the outskirts of Del Norte, he could see that weariness consumed her. It had been a long and tiring day. "You must be exhausted, Ms. St. John, and I'm pretty worn out myself," he said quietly as he glanced at his watch. "But I still need to get your statement about everything that happened today while the events are still fresh. Then I need to make sure you're safe for the evening."

"Please, call me Luann." She arched an eyebrow. "You don't think I'm safe at the bed-and-breakfast?"

Joaquin nodded. "Well, Susanna's a great hostess, but someone tried to kill you today. Twice. Let me think about this while we work through my report." He rubbed his chin with one hand as he drove. There was another bed-and-breakfast in town, but it was similar in size and structure to where she was already staying, and it wasn't going to be any safer if she moved from one to the other. Del Norte was small, and he didn't have a lot of options. He'd never had to put someone into protective custody before, but he didn't feel comfortable leaving Luann to her own devices after everything that had happened today. He glanced at her again, his thoughts whirling. He couldn't imagine putting her in the same cell where he put the drunks and teenaged troublemakers he'd arrested in the past, but he was tired, too, and no other solution was jumping to his mind.

It was already dark outside, and when they arrived at the police station, Joaquin did a quick parking job and escorted her inside the small building that housed the sheriff's office. There wasn't much to it. A large open bay with three desks was in the front, and in the back, he had an office separated by a large wall of glass. One door led to a bathroom and another to the jail in the back. A young officer with dark hair and eyes was sipping coffee and pinning up some notices on a bulletin board near the door. He was the only one there, although a police radio crackled in the background from a table under the window.

"Hey, boss," the young man nodded. "Sad news about Fabio." He reached down and patted Lobo, who had followed the two inside.

"Ricky." Joaquin greeted him and motioned to Luann. "This is Luann St. John. Luann, this is Ricky Trujillo one of my deputies."

"Ma'am." Henry smiled and touched his forehead as if he were wearing a hat and had tipped it at her. "It's nice to meet you." His expression turned somber. "Gary called. He said he finished giving your car the once-over and figures that it would cost more to fix than it's worth. He said the insurance company will probably total it out. He promised to help you deal with the rental car company tomorrow, if you want him to, that is. He's got his report all written up."

Luann sighed. "I figured as much, but his help would be welcome. Somehow, I'm going to need to get a replacement vehicle so I can get around."

Ricky nodded. "Gary said he has a friend over in Albuquerque that can probably help you. He comes to Del Norte every now and then to make deliveries and might be coming over tomorrow or the next day."

"Any news about the brakes?" Joaquin asked.

Ricky suddenly looked uncomfortable. He shuffled back and forth on his feet. "The brake line was definitely tampered with. He took pictures and said he wants you to stop by tomorrow so he can show you what he found."

Joaquin's gut tightened. So, it *had* been attempted murder. But who would want to kill Luann, and why? She swayed slightly on her feet, and he gently reached over and took her arm. "Steady." He motioned with his other hand. "Let's go to my office." He led her through the door and closed it behind them, then helped her sit in a worn burgundy-leather chair. Lobo lay down on a large gray-corduroy dog bed in the corner.

"Are you okay?" he asked softly.

"I will be," she mumbled. "I'm just not used to having people try to kill me. This has been quite the welcome."

"Understandable," Joaquin replied. "Although the fact that you've gotten someone's attention does give more credence to the idea that your dad was somehow on that plane after the robbery. I mean, if he wasn't, why would anyone be trying to stop your investigation?" He pulled off the oversized gloves and tossed them on his desk. "I have a couple of phone calls to make. If you could give me a minute or two, I'll be right back."

She nodded at him and he left her in his office with the door closed while he made two quick calls with his cell phone out in the bay and made a printed copy of the map he'd taken a picture of from Fabio's. Then he returned to his office, sat down behind his desk, and opened a laptop computer on his right and hit a few keys. He winced as he typed, forgetting that his fingers were a bit sore and singed from the fire. He saw notifications from Gary but closed his email app and opened the template for his official reports. "I'll take a look at Gary's pictures later," he said gently. "Right now, let's just get your statement and get you back to Susanna's so you can rest."

They spent the next hour going over the details surrounding her car accident, and then everything that had happened at Fabio's house. Joaquin took quite a few notes, even though he was pretty tired himself. This was an unusual case, and he wanted to make sure that he documented as much as possible so he didn't miss anything. He also wanted to share his report with his contact at the state investigation bureau, so once he was finished, he emailed a copy of the final report to his attention. By the time the interview was complete, he still hadn't worked out the best way to keep Luann safe. He leaned back in his chair.

"So, here's the thing. We don't really have a setup here for putting someone in protective custody, but we need you safe while we figure out what's going on and if what happened to Fabio is related to your father's case. I don't have a place for you here at the office, but I worked something out with Susanna on the phone a few minutes ago, so I can stay in the room next to yours for a few days while we continue the investigation. I haven't come up with a better idea, but if you have one, now is the time."

Luann sighed, relief evident on her features. "I wasn't sure what to do. I would appreciate having you nearby, but I hate to put you out."

"It's my job," Joaquin said as he stood and motioned toward the door. "And I'm not the least bit inconvenienced. Let's get you squared away. I'll give you a ride over there. Then tomorrow morning, we'll start fresh. You can show me those videos and we'll decide how to proceed."

Luann agreed and wearily followed him out the door and back into the car. It wasn't that far to the bed-and-breakfast, but she just didn't feel safe walking outside, even with the sheriff and his large dog by her side. Once they arrived, her skin prickled and she felt cold, as if someone was surreptitiously watching her. Was she still in danger?

She looked around carefully but didn't see any movement. Then something suddenly caught her eye near the corner of the gas station across the street. The store was closed, but it had some lighting around the front office door that spilled over and forced shadows into the recesses around the building. Was someone out there watching her, right now planning her demise? She wasn't sure if she'd seen a movement, a reflection or something else. All she knew was that they weren't alone, and she was in danger. A cold chill swept over her and she rubbed her arms. She couldn't remember ever feeling this scared and unsure.

"Are you okay?" Joaquin asked. Lobo appeared close beside him, and his ears pricked as he also looked toward the gas station.

"I thought I saw someone over there behind those pumps," she said, pointing.

"Go on inside," Joaquin said softly. "I'll go check it out."

She went up the steps but paused at the door and turned to see if he encountered anyone. Lobo seemed genuinely engaged in the search as well, and when the dog started barking, Luann quickly entered the foyer of the bed-and-breakfast, not waiting to see who or what they discovered.

A few minutes later, both Joaquin and Lobo returned, and entered the lobby where Luann was sitting on the couch. She jumped to her feet, anxious to hear his report. "Did you see anyone?"

"No, but there was definitely someone there. Lobo sniffed around quite a bit, but whoever it was probably saw us coming and drove off in a hurry. We heard a car leaving the area at a pretty fast clip. Unfortunately, we don't have cameras anywhere in town, so I don't have any way of following up to see who was out there. It could have been something totally unrelated, or it could have been a problem. We just don't know."

Luann's hands started shaking and she couldn't seem

to make them stop. She fidgeted with the strap on her purse, hoping to hide her discomfort. She was tired and stressed and smelled like a toasted marshmallow. She could also feel the allure of a warm bath calling her.

Joaquin noticed and nodded at Susanna, the proprietor of the house, who had been waiting quietly by the door for them to finish their conversation. She entered the room and handed him a hotel-like key along with a small bag of toiletries.

“Let’s get you settled,” Susanna said with a smile.

Luann led the way and opened the door to her room with her key, but Joaquin insisted that he check out the room first to make sure there were no surprises. He and Lobo came back into the hall a few moments later, declaring the room safe to enter.

“I checked the locks on your windows and you’re all set. Once you’re in there, lock the door behind you. If you have any trouble at all, just shout and I’ll come running.” He gave her a smile. “Don’t worry, Luann. We’ll get this sorted out.”

She gave him a tremulous smile. She didn’t feel as confident as he did but didn’t want to seem ungrateful for all of the help he was giving her either. “Thanks, Sheriff. I’ll see you for breakfast?”

“Yes, I’ll meet you downstairs at 8:00 a.m., and please, call me Joaquin. If you bring your laptop, you can show me those videos, too.”

“Perfect,” Luann replied. She locked the door behind herself as instructed and went straight to the bathroom and started to draw a bath. Steam and the smell of rose-scented bath salts filled the air. While she waited, she grabbed her cell phone.

"Mom? How are you doing today?"

"I'm hanging in there," her mother replied. "You know how it goes. I have my good days, and I have my bad ones. This one has been rather tough."

"I'm so sorry to hear that." Luann could hear the pain in her mother's voice. The cancer medications her mother had to take had a slew of side effects, which sometimes seemed to be even worse than the disease itself. Her mother didn't like to talk about her illness, however, and quickly brought the conversation back to Luann's mission.

"How goes your trip to Del Norte? Did you discover anything new?"

Luann paused. She didn't want to tell her mom about the attempts on her life. All that would do was worry her, and with the elder lady's bout with cancer taking the forefront, she sure didn't need anything else to stress about. Luann also didn't want to share the discouragement she was feeling after today. Was she strong enough to handle everything that was happening? Doubts and fears assailed her. She was a teacher at a community college. She didn't have a job that put her life in danger and wasn't used to being a target. However, if she didn't investigate, who would? Law enforcement in Las Cruces had made it clear that the case was closed. For Luann, just hearing her mother's voice bolstered her resolve. It was up to her to find answers. If she didn't push to discover the truth, her father's disappearance would never be resolved. Her mother would die without knowing the truth, and Luann would never have closure and be able to move on.

She instilled her voice with as much confidence as she could muster. "Well, Fabio wasn't able to help, but I did meet the local sheriff today. He's a nice man with a very large dog! Come to think of it, he's a big guy as well, so the two of them are well matched. Anyway, he's interested in helping me investigate the case, so I'm going to show him the videos tomorrow morning and we'll see what happens."

"That's encouraging!" her mother said with true enthusiasm in her voice. "In fact, isn't that the first real help you've received since you arrived up there?"

"Yes, he's the first one who has showed any interest."

They chatted a little longer, but Luann could hear the weariness threading through her mother's voice like a faint echo of pain she was trying to disguise. Reluctantly, Luann ended the call and set the phone on the small table beside her. The quiet in the room pressed in, amplifying the ache in her chest.

Before calling her mom, she had nearly convinced herself to abandon this mission altogether. She'd pictured herself packing her things, driving the long road back home, and pretending none of this had ever mattered. But she couldn't—not when her mother's health was slipping further each day, and time felt like sand draining too quickly through the hourglass.

The danger she now faced only deepened her conviction. Someone wanted her to stop, which meant she was on the right path. Every obstacle, every threat, whispered of truths long buried. She had to keep going, no matter the cost.

Her father's memory deserved that. Her mother deserved that. And maybe, just maybe, with the sheriff's help—his steady presence, his protective gaze—she would find the strength to uncover what had been hidden for so long.

Her quest was not just about answers. It was also about justice, and love.

SIX

"Pancakes are my favorite!"

Luann smiled at the little girl's exuberance and forked a couple of pancakes onto her own plate from the serving platter on the lazy Susan in the middle of the table. Susanna laid out a buffet of sorts on the table each morning as part of the bed-and-breakfast routine, and she always had great choices to whet a variety of appetites. "I like them, too. Do you want any syrup?"

The girl smiled and nodded, and Luann helped her pour a generous amount over her pancakes. She wasn't sure who the little girl belonged to, but she sure was a sweet thing with dark hair and eyes and a beautiful smile. Her hair was pulled back in a ponytail, and she was wearing jeans and a blue sweater. In the corner, Luann spied a pink backpack and lunchbox that looked like they had recently been packed and were ready to go. They were the only two people at the breakfast table, and Luann figured the child didn't belong to Susanna because she'd never seen her before during her stay, not to mention the fact that Susanna and her husband were probably both in their sixties. Maybe there was another guest that had just checked in last night?

"My name is Luann," she said as she poured syrup over her own pancakes. "What's yours?"

"I'm Camila," the little girl said between bites.

"So, the two of you have met," said a male voice from the entryway. "I was hoping you would."

Luann turned and gave Joaquin a smile as he entered the room. "So, does this little lady belong to you?"

"She does indeed." He came up behind his daughter and gave her a kiss on the top of her head. "Getting enough to eat there, sunshine?" he asked as he touched her nose playfully.

"Sure, Daddy. Did you know Ms. Luann likes pancakes, too?"

"I didn't." He reached over and grabbed a strawberry from the serving dish. "But that's a good thing to know. It looks like Ms. Susanna has put out quite a spread of great foods to choose from." He popped the berry into his mouth. "Yum!" He grabbed his own plate and started piling it high with a variety of selections from the lazy Susan, just as Susanna came back in carrying a new plate of freshly sautéed hash browns with bits of green chile and Monterey Jack cheese liberally sprinkled throughout.

"I thought I heard you come in," Susanna said with a grin. She was a grandmotherly type and eyed his full plate with satisfaction and pride. "I'm glad to see you're filling up. We can't have the sheriff feeling weak and fainting from lack of food when he's staying at my place. What would people think?"

"Agreed," Joaquin said as he liberally added some of the new potatoes to his plate. Susanna laughed and went into the kitchen but came back a moment later with her apron gone and a set of keys jingling in her hand.

"Alright, my little *tamale*, it's time to go."

Camila laughed, shoved the last bite of pancake into her mouth, and took her plate into the kitchen. A moment later, she returned and grabbed the backpack and lunchbox as she quickly gave her daddy a sticky kiss and followed Susanna out.

"Have a great day at school, Camila," Joaquin called out.

"I didn't know you had such a precious daughter," Luann commented. "Is she your only child?"

"Yes, I only have the one. She is precious, isn't she?" He shook his head. "I don't know what I'd do without her."

"Is Susanna taking her to kindergarten?"

"Preschool," Joaquin confirmed. "She'll go to kindergarten next year. Her birthday was too close to the cut-off date."

"It takes a village," Luann commented as she poured herself some more juice.

"Susanna has been great. She and Ted, her husband, don't have any children, so they've been helping me out ever since my wife left."

"Where did your wife go?"

Joaquin's face suddenly shrouded, and Luann instantly knew she had broached a subject that was still painful to the sheriff. "Who knows? She found another man and left me and Camila behind around two years ago."

"I'm so sorry," Luann said softly. "I had no idea."

He shrugged. "I've been struggling with having a work-life balance ever since, and Susanna and Ted have been great friends. They've stepped up and treat Camila like a grandchild, and of course, the little imp just eats it up. That's another reason why it's not a hardship to stay here to keep an eye on you and make sure you're safe. Camila already feels comfortable here and has a little bed in their apartment that she uses when she sleeps over." He took another swig of coffee and motioned to her laptop that she had placed beside her on the table. "Ready to show me your videos?"

"I am," Luann confirmed. She was glad she was getting to know the sheriff a little better, especially since they would be working closely together. She set aside her plate, opened her laptop, and hit a few keys on her keyboard to open the files. "I got these from a friend who works at the police department. The first few are the original surveillance videos from the jewelry store." She pushed Play and watched as her father, wearing a navy business suit, opened the wire-mesh screen that blocked the front door when the store was closed and unlocked the front door of the jewelry store. He was obviously in a good mood and was jingling his keys. He was a tall man, with clean-cut features and short dark hair. The time stamp showed the video was twenty years old and had been recorded at 7:36 a.m. He entered and flipped the Closed sign to Open before disappearing inside.

"So there wasn't a camera inside the store?" Joaquin asked.

"No, the owner didn't want his customers to feel uncomfortable, so he always claimed the front door camera was enough. There was a camera at the back door, too, but nobody entered or exited from that door on the day my father disappeared."

Luann closed that file and opened the next one. This video also showed the front of the store again and had a time stamp of 12:13 p.m. Her dad was closing the store in this video, and another man stood off to the left, waiting for him as he went through the procedures of locking up the glass door and mesh screen. It was easy to see the figure to the side was that of a man, but he was wearing a large cowboy hat that covered his face. He was also wearing dark pants, brown leather loafers, and a white shirt with a light blue tie and navy jacket. There was a gold ring on his left hand that was only visible because he kept his hands on his hips for most of the video.

"Your father's behavior has changed," Joaquin offered. "His body language is different. He seems subdued now instead of happy like he was at the beginning of the day."

"Agreed." Luann nodded, pleased that the sheriff had noticed. "His motions are stilted. I tried to tell that to the police when we reviewed these, but they said that could be his normal behavior, and they dismissed it." She tilted her head. "To be fair, I didn't get to see these until I was an adult. All of this happened when I was eight years old. By the time I saw the videos, the case was cold, and law enforcement was so busy with their new cases that no one wanted to take it on. They said strange behavior wasn't enough to reopen the case."

Joaquin nodded, an understanding look on his face. "That happens pretty frequently. A lot of departments don't even have a cold case squad. They can barely handle the cases on their current caseload. Funding is a common problem." He motioned at the computer. "So, what happened next?"

Luann grimaced. "The owner came by around 3:00 p.m. and noticed that the store was still closed, and almost two million dollars in diamonds was missing. He called the police, but they didn't have any leads until later." She pushed some hair behind her ear. "There's not much to that video. It just shows him arriving, and then the police showing up." She hit a few more keys on the laptop. "Later, law enforcement found that a skydiving plane was taken from the general aviation tarmac on the same day. They had this video."

She started the recording that showed a small airfield with several small planes parked near a hanger. The film was grainy, but as they watched, three men walked toward the plane, two in front, with a third man behind them. The man bringing up the rear had on a hat similar to the hat the man was wearing near the jewelry store, and his face was still not visible. In this video, the man was wearing jeans and a button-down shirt, so despite the cowboy hat, if it was the same man, he had changed the rest of his clothing.

"That's the one that I think looks like my dad." She pointed to the man on the left. "He's not wearing the same clothes, and I think that's why the detectives dismissed this video. To me, that man has the same body shape and movements as my dad, but the police couldn't explain why he would have changed, and the camera never gets a really clear shot of his face. To them, that man didn't seem under duress either, so they dismissed this video out of hand and said the two events weren't related. To this day, that man has remained unidentified." She pointed to the other man. "That one is clearly blond and is the pilot known to take out that plane for the skydiver team. His name is Bill Gladstone. His body was the only one recovered from the plane wreckage."

The video showed the men walking toward the plane but then panned away before it showed anyone actually getting on. After a few seconds, the video verified the plane taxiing down the runway. There was no sign of the other two men. "I really think that man in the video is my dad, and the other man with the hat is the same one that forced him to lock up the jewelry store. To me, the hats look the same. But the detective I spoke with who handled the case dismissed the video, and said there wasn't enough there to prove that it was them with the pilot. After all, when the plane crashed, the pilot was alone." She closed her laptop with a snap. "According to the police, there's no proof of anything except that the diamonds are missing, and my father, who was responsible for them, had disappeared."

Joaquin rubbed his chin with his hand. "And what do you think?"

"I think that my dad did take the diamonds, but that he was forced by the man with the hat to steal them. Maybe he was threatened. I don't know, but he wasn't a thief. I also think the guy with the hat made my dad get on the plane, and somehow, the two of them got off the plane before it crashed, or their bodies just were never found and are up here somewhere in the New Mexican mountains." She paused. "I think my dad was kidnapped, and he didn't willingly take part in the theft."

Joaquin was silent for a few minutes, apparently digesting everything she'd shown and told him. Finally, he spoke. "Was there any evidence that the plane stopped anywhere between when they took off and the crash in the mountains?"

Luann shook her head. "Not according to the flight plan. That's all I have."

Joaquin tilted his head. "Okay. So where do you want to go from here?"

Luann let out a breath she didn't even know she was holding. Joaquin hadn't said, "Forget it, I'm not helping you." In fact, he seemed willing to continue the investigation. Still, she had to be sure.

"So, you're going to help me?"

Joaquin frowned. "Of course. I thought I already said so."

Luann digested that for a moment and blew out a breath in relief. "I'm just surprised. I was afraid that after I showed you the videos, you'd think there wasn't enough there and you'd give up on the search."

Joaquin shook his head. "Sounds like some others have let you down, but when I say something, I mean it. My word is my bond." He smiled back. He had a really nice smile. It lit up his entire face and changed his countenance completely. Even his eyes seemed to dance when he smiled.

Luann smiled back. She couldn't help herself. "Good to know! Well, I started by trying to talk to anyone that might have been around the area twenty years ago, but I haven't gotten very far. So far, either people don't know anything about it or they're not willing to discuss it. If that didn't provide any new leads, I was hoping to do some wilderness camping and check out the crash site. I know it's a bit cold outside, but this is the first time I've had the chance to get some time off from work and come up here to search. I want to see if I can find any clues at all that prove my dad was on the flight."

"Have you read the crash scene reports from the National Transportation Safety Board?"

"Yes, but I didn't see any proof about my dad one way or the other. The reports were pretty sterile."

Joaquin rubbed his chin. He hoped for Luann's sake that what she thought had happened to her father was the actual truth, but in his experience, people were quick to disappoint the ones they loved. Images of his own wife and her betrayal instantly sprang to mind, but he tried to squash those and focus on the positive. Despite his ex-wife's abandonment, he had a lovely little girl. Camila was the light of his life, and he could never regret the events that had brought her to him, however painful. Still, he wondered about Luann's father. He'd obviously never met the man, so it was hard to know for sure, but he hoped for Luann's sake that he wasn't just a scoundrel who had robbed his employer and lived out the rest of his days sipping cold drinks on a tropical beach somewhere, leaving his family alone to wonder and fend for themselves.

It didn't seem possible that people could be that cruel to each other, his own situation notwithstanding, but he'd seen some terrible things as a police officer.

But God had carried him through each and every situation he had been through, both on the job and in his personal life.

He didn't know how people dealt with horrible things without God in their lives. His own faith had been and continued to be the foundation of his life. Without it, he wasn't sure he could get up in the morning. He hoped Luann had the same faith that he depended upon but didn't feel comfortable bringing it up just yet. After all, he'd only met her yesterday.

He pulled his thoughts back to Luann and the story of

her father's disappearance. He doubted that visiting the crash site would yield anything fruitful, but despite his skepticism, someone was determined to harm Luann. What was the connection? Had the men hidden the missing jewels somewhere, hoping to come back later and retrieve them? Had the pilot been in on the theft? Or had the plane had nothing at all to do with the diamonds? Whatever the case, he had promised to help Luann and was determined to make good on his promise.

A door slammed, and heavy steps coming into the kitchen along with Lobo's barking made Joaquin suddenly stand and protectively block Luann from whoever was heading in their direction.

"So, you're the one who killed Fabio?" an angry male voice said from the doorway.

Joaquin put up his hands, instantly recognizing Carlos Sanchez, the son of a local rancher. "Easy there, Carlos. What are you talking about?"

"I'm talking about that woman sitting behind you! She killed Fabio!" Carlos's face was red from emotion, and his voice rose in pitch as he yelled and waved his arms in a threatening motion.

"You're wrong," Joaquin replied, purposefully keeping his voice calm and low. In his experience, it was easier to defuse a difficult situation if he stayed levelheaded. "I was there with her the entire time. Fabio was dead when we arrived and had been for several hours. Then someone tried to kill both of us with the fire. Ms. St. John had nothing to do with Fabio's death. She was just at the wrong place at the wrong time." He turned and glanced quickly at Luann, who had shrunk back closer to the wall. He swiveled to Carlos quickly, in case the young man continued his onslaught. Carlos was a hothead, and Joaquin had arrested him several times for drinking and driving, drug use and some petty theft when the young man was in high school. Now Carlos was in his early twenties and worked at his father's ranch, but he still caused trouble sometimes and was one of the regulars Joaquin kept his eye on.

"Fabio was my friend," Carlos said hotly. "And if that woman you're protecting doesn't leave town immediately, I'm going to make sure she pays!"

SEVEN

Carlos took a step forward, and Joaquin did as well, although the lawman continued to keep his stance calm and nonthreatening. He didn't want Carlos to feel challenged or encouraged to escalate what was already a very tense situation. He'd dealt with the younger man a variety of ways over the past few years and found that a peaceful approach usually helped reduce the anger and frustration Carlos emitted. "I'm sorry Fabio is dead, but Ms. St. John didn't even know Fabio. She just wanted to ask him a few questions about the history of the area, but she never even got the chance. I promise you, she did nothing to hurt him." He tilted his head. "I didn't know you two were friends."

"I was doing some work for Fabio on the side," Carlos admitted. "We hung out sometimes."

Joaquin nodded. "When we went up to his place yesterday, we saw a large worktable and a map that looked like he was doing some exploring. Do you know anything about that?"

"No," Carlos said quickly, but Joaquin noticed his eyes widened a bit and he clenched his hands. Was Carlos lying? He didn't spend enough time around the man to know for sure, but his body language suggested he knew more than he was admitting.

Why would Carlos lie?

It must have something to do with Luann and her investigation, or he wouldn't even be there. But what was the connection?

Was Carlos responsible for the fire at the cabin? He'd seen him there yesterday, one of the crowd watching as the firefighters battled the flames, but he hadn't gotten the chance to talk to him.

Despite Carlos's history with drugs and alcohol, he had a hard time believing the young man was capable of attempted murder. He'd known Carlos's father, Levi, for years, and had a good relationship with the rancher. Granted, Carlos was a hothead, but a murderer? That seemed far-fetched.

Del Norte was a small village though. Joaquin had a hard time imagining *any* of the residents could be capable of taking another's life. He met Carlos's eyes. "Well, just to be clear, Ms. St. John had nothing to do with Fabio's murder, or with the fire. She's only going to be in town for a few days. While she's here, I need you to stay away from her."

Carlos blew out a breath, and the muscles around his neck seemed to bunch and bulge, but he finally nodded and turned on his heel and left. Joaquin made sure he was gone, then turned back to Luann. "Sorry about that. He's a hothead, but I don't think he's responsible for the attempts on your life yesterday."

"I saw him there, behind the police tape," Luann admitted. "He was glaring at me, like he was blaming me for something. Now I understand why he was so upset."

She hugged herself and rubbed her arms. "Do you think he's the one who was waiting outside the bed-and-breakfast last night?"

"It's entirely possible," Joaquin agreed. "He clearly wanted to express himself, and he might have needed the evening to get up his courage for this confrontation." He shifted. "I think he'll leave us alone. Are you ready to do some research?"

"Sure. Where are we headed?"

Joaquin motioned toward the east with his hand. "I was thinking the town library should be our first stop."

She looked at him skeptically. "You have a library here?"

Joaquin smiled, not surprised to hear the doubt in her voice. "It's not much of one, but it works for our little community." He raised an eyebrow. "Nobody mentioned it to you before?"

She shook her head. "No, people haven't been real forthcoming when I start asking questions. I guess folks were a little concerned about my motives. They don't know me, or my family."

Joaquin shook his head. "I have to admit I'm a bit surprised, but I get it. The folks out here do value their privacy."

She followed him out to his squad car. Lobo had been lying on a mat on the front porch, but when they left, the dog got up, stretched, and followed them out. Joaquin opened up the car door to the back seat and Lobo jumped in, ready for the next step of their adventure.

Less than five minutes later, Joaquin parked in front of the small-town library. It wasn't much of a library but was actually just the back room of one of the shops that had previously been the town's newspaper office. The newspaper had closed years ago and been replaced with an antique store, but no one had ever cleaned out the newspaper archives, and over time, locals had added several bookshelves and donated books until the "library" had grown into a small, unmanned source for town history, book swaps and other information. The three entered through the front door and Joaquin tapped the brim of his new cowboy hat at the proprietor as they walked through to the library entrance. He'd lost his favorite hat during the fire, but thankfully, he'd had this backup and had picked it up at his office the night before. "Morning, Josie."

"Good morning, Sheriff," an elderly lady responded. Lobo was quick to approach the woman and nuzzled her hand, expecting and receiving a rubbing of the ears that pleased the dog immensely. There was a dog bed next to the cash register, and Lobo settled in, a welcomed and regular guest in the store.

"So, what do you think we'll find here?" Luann asked as she followed him into the back room.

Joaquin shrugged. "You have the date of the crash, so I thought we'd look at the newspapers from around that time and see if we can glean anything new."

Joaquin flipped on the light as they entered. The "library" had about twenty banker boxes of old newspapers along the back wall, all labeled, as well as six floor-to-ceiling bookshelves and other shelving along the other two walls, all filled to the rim with books. A table and two chairs sat in the middle of the room, and the air smelled musty, and although everything was neat and orderly, a fine layer of dust coated the aged wooden shelves and the boxes and books. It was obvious that some sections were well used, such as the fiction and romance shelves, while others, mostly old cookbooks and other nonfiction titles, got less use.

Joaquin loved the old room. It was peaceful, and the smell actually reminded him of his grandfather's home where he had spent quite a bit of time growing up. He pushed away the memories and made his way to the boxes that held the newspapers. "They only published the local paper once a week between the years of 1983 and 2009. After that, it went out of business. I'm not even sure they have copies of every edition, but it's worth a look." He looked at the labels that advertised the dates of the contents and pulled out the 2005 box. Inside there were twelve issues of the small newspaper, as well as a few receipts and a bundle of expenditure reports. "What date did all of this happen?"

"Thursday, July 14, 2005," Luann replied, joining him by the box. He handed her the issues for the following few weeks. "The paper was only published weekly on Saturday nights. Why don't you start with these and I'll take a look at the later editions that came out during the following months? There might be some mention of the crash and subsequent investigation."

"Deal." Luann took a seat, and he sat across from her with the remaining papers from 2005. He didn't expect much—it was an inconsequential paper after all, but the small press was a good place to start.

"Here's one!" Luann said excitedly as she found an article on the second page of the July 17, 2005 paper. She scanned the article quickly, but as Joaquin watched, her beginning elation began to dwindle. "There's not much here. The author confirms that only the pilot's body was found, and that the cause of the crash is unknown, pending investigation." She pushed some of her hair back behind her ear. "A couple of locals were interviewed who saw the flames and heard the crash, but it was apparently in a pretty remote area. There's not much else to it."

"Well, it takes a while for details to emerge, even in larger crashes. The investigators have to come in, find that little black box from the flight deck, and then put all of the pieces back together. Since this wasn't a commercial plane from one of the big airlines, it got a lot less press. Let's continue checking some of the later editions."

Luann snapped a picture of the article she was reading, then stored the paper and pulled out the next. She didn't find anything else until seven weeks later when the author reported that the crash was deemed an accident attributed to pilot error. Joaquin read the article she showed him, then showed her one he had found from four months after the crash. It didn't add much to the story except to explain that the investigation had been closed by the NTSB.

"Well, that didn't yield much," Luann said, her shoulders slumped. "I was hoping for more." She motioned toward the 2005 box. "I think Mr. Sanchez's prize stallion got most of the press during this time period. That horse he purchased back in early 2005 seems to have really been a winner. It pushed almost everything else off the first page for three different editions."

Joaquin smiled. "Welcome to small-town America. Livestock up here is a really big deal. Plane crashes don't happen very often, thankfully, but since no one who lived nearby was involved, the paper tended to focus on local events and news. That's what folks wanted to read about."

Luann put the lid back on the box. "I get it. Is the publisher still alive?"

"Nope," Joaquin answered. "He died back in 2009. That's why the paper stopped being printed. No one wanted to take it over. These days, it's all about websites anyway. Not many people even read the paper anymore, at least in these parts. I haven't even looked at an *Albuquerque Journal* in years. I really don't even know if they're still publishing it or not."

Luann picked up her phone and looked at the picture of the article. "The author mentions two people who saw or heard the crash—that horse owner, Mr. Sanchez and a Mr. Ortega. Maybe we could visit them to see if they can add anything to the story?" She grimaced. "I know it's a long shot, but I'm running out of ideas."

"Mr. Sanchez is Carlos's father. He runs a ranch where people can rent horses, go on camping trips, that kind of thing." Luann's eyes widened but Joaquin put up his hands. "No, he's nothing like his son. He's a good man and has been a pillar of this community for years." He rubbed his chin. "I could be wrong, but I think 2005 is around the time that Sanchez moved up here and set up his ranch." The two started walking out of the library and back into the store section of the building. "Ortega used to live in town, but he died a few years back. I'm not sure he would have been much help anyway. He was always pretty friendly, but he was also rather odd."

"Odd how?" Luann asked as Lobo came up beside her.

"Odd as in his mind tended to wander when you talked to him. He had a hard time staying focused, and I think he ended up with dementia. But he was a sweet guy, once you got to know him. He lived in Del Norte for quite a while and seemed to have a new conspiracy theory to share every week. Back in the day, he used to be a volunteer firefighter, so he might have participated in the search and rescue operation, if there was one. That's probably why he was mentioned in the story." He furrowed his brow. "Who was the author of the article?"

"Catia Reyes."

Joaquin nodded. "She's a local, too. We can swing by her place. She's a homebody these days."

"Sounds good." They made it to the front porch of the store, the weathered boards creaking under their steps, when a flicker of movement to the right snagged Luann's attention. Her stomach tightened. "Is that a rifle over there?" she whispered, pointing toward the shadowy edge of the nearby parking lot.

The answer came instantly. A deafening crack split the air and a bullet tore into the wooden doorframe just inches from her head. Splinters sprayed her cheek, and the impact was so close she could smell the acrid burn of fresh gunpowder. Her gasp stuck in her throat.

Before her mind could register the danger, Joaquin's instincts must have taken over. He shoved her down to the porch, his body covering hers like a shield. The weight of him, solid and protective, pressed her into the rough planks as her heart hammered.

"Stay down," he ordered, his voice a raw whisper edged with urgency. He dragged a heavy wooden chair across the porch, wedging it as a barrier between her and the open lot. Then he shifted, rising slightly, preparing to return fire.

Luann's hand shot out, clutching his shirt with desperate strength. "What about you?" Her voice trembled.

"This is my job." His eyes locked on hers, steady, resolute. "You'll be safe here. I've got to stop the shooter before they come closer." She could tell he was about to rise and go after the gunman. The thought terrified her.

"It's not worth your life!" she hissed, fear tightening her chest.

But he was already moving, crouching low behind the porch's support pole, weapon drawn, and scanning. Their eyes met again across the tense space, his gaze fierce, hers wide with terror.

"I'll be back," he promised, softer now, meant only for her.

And then he was gone—slipping down the steps, swallowed by shadow and danger, leaving her pressed against the porch, pulse thundering.

Luann gripped the edge of the chair, knuckles white, every muscle taut. The silence between shots was worse than the crack of the rifle. Where was he? Had the gunman already taken aim again? She couldn't breathe, couldn't move, terrified that the next sound she heard would be Joaquin's body hitting the ground.

Her mind screamed at her to run, to hide, to abandon this reckless mission. But her heart clung to one impossible truth. She couldn't quit. Not now.

And what about Joaquin? He wasn't just a sheriff doing his job. He was her shield. And if she lost him out there in the darkness, she wasn't sure she'd survive it.

EIGHT

Joaquin made his way to the street, finding cover first behind a piñon, and then behind a sedan parked near the entrance. Another shot rang out, but this one was definitely aimed at him, which was his goal. He wanted to make himself the target, to keep the shooter focused on him instead of Luann. He was a law enforcement officer. It was his job to protect her, and he was determined to do so and chase down this shooter before he was able to hurt her. That included drawing fire away from the porch where she was lying prone behind that wooden chair and railing. She made a difficult target now, which the shooter also seemed to realize. A bullet ravaged the metal near his shoulder, and he crouched down farther, then moved again behind a different vehicle, hoping to get a glimpse of the person firing at him or at least some clue as to his identity. He wondered fleetingly who the shooter might be, and did a mental inventory of those who had both the personality and the skill, or lack of it, to shoot at another human being.

Suddenly, Joaquin heard a vehicle door slam and an engine roar to life. He chanced a look around the car's bumper that he was using for a shield, and saw a silver pickup starting to move near where they had first seen the rifle. The truck's tires squealed against the pavement as the driver sped away. Joaquin stood, still using the car for cover, trying to get a better view of the truck. It was a newer model, but he didn't recognize the vehicle and couldn't get a good look at the license plate.

He hadn't seen the shooter either—all he'd been able to make out was that it was probably a man of average height and weight, wearing a baseball cap, a brown leather jacket and jeans. He pulled out his phone and called the office, then provided a description of what he knew and ordered his deputies to go after the truck. He doubted they would find anything, but they had to try. Was the shooter a stranger from out of town, or had someone local gotten a new truck? He believed it was probably the former, but he ordered them to take a look at Carlos Sanchez as well, and to make sure he had a viable alibi for the time of the shooting. He still didn't think Carlos was the perpetrator, but he needed to be sure.

He quickly made his way back up to the porch and reached out to help Luann to her feet. "Are you okay?"

"I'm fine." She took his hand, and a tingle went up his arm. Their eyes met for a moment, and he was struck by how pretty she was, even in this moment of distress and fear. Her deep-set brown eyes showed a vulnerability that spoke to him, and he felt the urge to hold her and soothe away her fear.

What was he thinking?

He chastised himself immediately, released her hand, and took a step back. He had been burned once before when his wife had left him. He would not open himself up to another relationship. It was too painful. Besides, he had a daughter to think about. And Luann wasn't even a local. She would discover what she could about her father and then return to her normal life in an entirely different city in New Mexico. There were a hundred reasons why he shouldn't be attracted to this lady or even think about having any sort of relationship with her.

And yet he was attracted to her and couldn't keep his mind from playing the what-if game with a variety of different scenarios in his head. If nothing else, Joaquin was honest with himself about the emotions suddenly swamping him. He might not want to feel anything for this lovely lady, but he couldn't deny the sentiments were there. He couldn't fight the warmth he felt when Luann smiled at him, or the happiness that swept over him when he knew he was about to be near her again. He would just have to tamp those feelings down for the next few days until she went back home. At that point, he could try to put her out of his mind and get back to his day-to-day job of enforcing the law and caring for his young daughter. That was enough. It would have to be.

"I've got my two deputies out looking for the shooter," he said quietly as he shifted from one foot to the other. "But I didn't recognize the truck, and there are a hundred different places to hide out here, so I'm not sure they'll have much success in finding it. They'll report back if they see anything."

Luann's face was still a bit pale, despite her valiant effort to appear unflustered. "Do you need to go, too?"

"What I need to do is stay near to you to make sure you're safe. The deputies are good at their jobs and can handle the search." She reached down and petted Lobo, and Joaquin thought it was great that his dog seemed to agree that staying close to Luann was a good idea. She seemed to sway a bit on her feet, and Joaquin quickly put his arm around her and led her to his car. She fit perfectly beside him.

He tried not to notice.

He got her inside and Lobo jumped in the back seat. A few minutes later, they were parked in front of Gary's garage. Luann's car was up on a rack in one of the two bays. They quickly entered the building and had Gary close the large garage door behind them, just to be sure no one could see them well enough to take another shot at them. After the door was closed, Gary continued wiping his hands on a towel as he approached, giving them both a questioning smile. He was an older man with very little hair, and he wore grease-stained coveralls and wire-rimmed glasses. "I'm glad ya'll stopped by, but what's the deal with the door?"

"Someone just took a shot at us in front of the library," Joaquin explained.

Gary's aged face registered his surprise as he stuffed the rag in his pocket and moved his hands to his hips. "That's crazy! Who would shoot someone in Del Norte, and why?"

"That's what I'm trying to figure out," Joaquin said quietly. "It was a silver Ford F-150, and a pretty new model." He paused a moment. "Do you know if Carlos Sanchez has a new truck?"

Gary thought about it for a moment, then replied, "Not that I know of. He was still driving that black Honda the last time I saw him, but that was a couple of weeks ago. You know, the one with the fuel pump that keeps getting recalled? I've already replaced it for him twice."

Joaquin rubbed his chin. "Know anybody else who might be driving a new silver truck around these parts?" If anybody paid attention to cars in the local area, it was Gary. He had a love for anything on wheels.

Gary tilted his head but then shook his head. "Nope." He motioned to Luann. "I'm sure sorry you're having all of these problems in our little town. Normally, we're a real nice bunch."

Luann smiled at him but said nothing, as if he wasn't convincing her. Joaquin couldn't blame her after witnessing for himself everything that had happened to her over the past twenty-four hours. He wondered if she was scared enough to give up her quest, or if she would push on. She still seemed pale, but he could see an inner strength in her now that hadn't been visible before. It was a good sign, and for better or worse, made him even more attracted to her.

"You don't believe me, hmm?" Gary asked, smiling back at Luann. He pulled a set of keys from his pocket and held them out to her. "These are for you. Your new rental car is waiting for you outside."

Luann's eyes widened. "Are you serious?"

Gary laughed at her expression. "Absolutely. I told Ricky I knew someone over in Albuquerque at the rental car place who would help us out. They delivered it a few minutes ago. They even gave you an upgrade without any additional charges, and their heartfelt apology. That little red Camry out there belongs to you for the duration of your stay."

She took the keys and pocketed them with a new level of appreciation and animation in her expression. "Thank you so much. That's a load off my mind."

Gary smiled and motioned for both of them to follow him under her car that was securely strapped to the rack. He pointed to the brake line by the rear axle. "Well, that was the good news. Here's the bad news." He made a sweeping motion to the wheel area. "Here's your problem with this car. Someone nicked the brake line—I would imagine with something like a wire or bolt cutter tool. The hoses on this car are made with reinforced rubber and are designed to withstand a great deal of pressure, so the damage had to be planned." He pointed. "See, here's the tube where the hydraulic fluid goes to the brakes. It was probably a slow leak, and they were nicked on both sides of the car." He turned toward Luann again. "Did you notice the warning light when you started the car, or feel like the brakes were a bit mushy before you started driving?"

She nodded. "Both, but I was pretty flustered and didn't really think about it since my mind was elsewhere. When I saw the light, I figured it had to be a mistake since the car was so new. I should have been paying more attention. But even if I had been, I don't know what I would have done about it. I'm not very mechanical."

Gary nodded. "Well, the important part is that you're safe now. Just to make sure, I did a quick safety check of the Camry they sent over and didn't find any issues. You should be good to go."

Luann didn't know if it was the stress of the situation, or just Gary's amazing kindness, but she reached over and gave him a heartfelt hug, despite the fact that she had just met the man and he was wearing very dirty coveralls. "Thank you. I really appreciate you going so far out of your way to help me." She stepped back.

Gary blushed and stammered as he spoke but looked pleased with her reaction. "You're welcome, ma'am."

Even with Gary's kindness, Luann still had a knot of fear in her stomach that twisted relentlessly as the events of the last twenty-four hours played over and over in her mind. Fabio was dead, and someone was continuing to attempt to take her life as well. Should she quit? Was finding out the truth about her father worth her life?

Questions spun in her mind. Despite everything, she couldn't quite figure out why someone would care about the facts surrounding her father's disappearance if he hadn't gotten on the plane that crashed near Del Norte. It mattered to her because of her abandonment issues and her desire to put her mother's mind at ease. But why would anyone else care what had become of her father? She'd heard that the insurance company had paid off her father's employer for the value of the missing diamonds, so she doubted he was concerned about anyone digging into the case, and even so, he was back in Las Cruces, still running his jewelry store. She'd had no contact with him at all over the past twenty years. She couldn't think of anyone else who would care one way or the other about her quest for answers—unless the perpetrator was still alive, and living in Del Norte…

A cold chill swept up her spine. She had no idea who the thief who had forced her father onto the plane was, or what had become of him. But could that criminal be living nearby, determined to protect his identity? She only had the grainy video from the crime scene as a guide. She doubted she could prove anyone's guilt with the measly evidence she had acquired, and law enforcement had closed the case years ago. Even if the guilty party had ended up in the area after the crash, he'd probably changed his looks and moved to another state or country years ago. Not to mention the fact that he would now be twenty years older and had undoubtedly changed over the years. Luann doubted the fear of being identified was at the root of the attacks against her. No, the perpetrator probably disappeared with the diamonds long ago and was living it up in some country that didn't allow extradition.

Then who was behind Fabio's death and the attempts on her life? Was finding out the truth worth risking her life? This question kept popping to the forefront of her mind. She wasn't sure what the right answer was, but she did know that if she let Him, God would show her the right path forward. She said a silent prayer, asking God for guidance and help deciding what her next move should be.

She followed Joaquin out to his car and gave Lobo a friendly pat before the dog jumped in the back seat again. Then, as she turned to Joaquin, she felt a strengthening of purpose and warmth sweep over her that calmed her. God was already answering her prayer and bolstering her spirit and resolve. She suddenly knew without a doubt that continuing the investigation was the right thing to do, despite the hardships. She also felt like God was using these difficulties to help make her stronger and to develop her faith. Looking back, she realized she had let fear and abandonment issues make decisions for her when times got tough. Regardless of what she discovered here in Del Norte, it was time to grow and put those feelings behind her.

She glanced over at Joaquin, who gave her a smile, and she considered the little she knew about his past. He and his daughter had been abandoned by his wife, yet here he was, moving forward with determination and a strength of character she saw displayed again and again as she got to know him. Her respect for him went up a notch as she really considered his situation. Joaquin was an admirable man.

She pulled herself out of her musings. "So, do we leave the Camry here, or do you want to take it?" she asked as she pulled out her new keys. Joaquin had made it clear that he was going to stick by her as they visited the next few contacts, and his caring and support bolstered her even further. He seemed to be a gentle giant, yet sometimes she could see a sadness in his expression that made her want to reach out and help him, especially since he was doing so much for her. It was obvious that his wife's departure had scarred him deeply, and she could definitely empathize with his feelings. Abandonment was a difficult emotion to come to terms with. After all, here she was in a strange place with people shooting at her, all because her father had abandoned her twenty years ago.

She studied Joaquin closely. She wasn't looking for a relationship, but she had to admit, he was easy on the eyes. It was crazy to be noticing, but admiring his attributes did take her mind off her own troubles. He was very muscular, with the body of a man who was no stranger to physical labor, and his features were strong and attractive. His chin was firm and his eyes intense and filled with intelligence and caring. His hair was jet black and cut short, and framed his face perfectly, and his brown skin showed both his heritage and his time out in the New Mexican sun. He was a "tall sack of groceries," as her best friend from college would often say when she noticed a good-looking man, but it wasn't only his appearance that Luann found attractive. She also enjoyed his playful banter and friendly protective spirit. She knew instinctively that he would never abandon her. Although she hadn't dated in quite a while and definitely wasn't looking for romance, she couldn't deny the feelings that made her heart beat just a little bit faster when Joaquin glanced her way.

Joaquin's voice broke into her thoughts. "Let's take my cruiser. We'll swing by later and pick up the Camry after we've talked to some of the people on the list." He closed the door behind his dog and motioned for her to get into the front seat of the police car as he took the seat behind the wheel.

A few minutes later, they were on the road, heading toward Catia Reyes's house, the author who had penned the newspaper articles they had discovered at the library.

Luann loved the mountain terrain and leaned into the seat, relaxing for the first time that day. She glanced into the sideview mirror, then suddenly sat up straight, her heart pounding against her chest. "Is that silver truck that just pulled in behind us the same one you saw disappear this morning after the shooting?"

NINE

"Looks like the same one to me," Joaquin said as he pressed on the accelerator. He quickly grabbed his two-way radio and called in to his two deputies and reported the situation, then focused on his driving. The truck was big and bulky and had a much larger engine than his little sedan. He glanced along the road both behind and in front of him and was glad that they were currently the only two vehicles on the roadway. He certainly didn't want any other civilians caught in the crossfire. Having Luann in danger once again was more than enough. Still, he was glad he had chosen to stick by her instead of abandoning her to whatever fate this criminal had planned for her. Her life was obviously still at risk, and he would do everything in his power to protect her.

The silver truck surged and was suddenly right up behind them. With a sickening crunch of metal, the pickup rammed them from behind. The cruiser lunged forward, and Joaquin struggled to keep it under control and on the road. He glanced over at Luann, who, eyes rounded, was grabbing the handle above the door and her seat belt so hard that her hands were turning white.

"Hold on," he encouraged as he slammed his foot down

on the gas pedal. The car surged forward, and the two vehicles raced down the winding road, taking the turns way too fast. The wheels and rubber squealed as they got farther and farther away from Del Norte, and Joaquin struggled to keep the cruiser on the asphalt as he sped around the turns.

Suddenly, the truck was right behind them once again and slammed into their rear with a huge amount of force, pushing their car precariously close to a drainage ditch much like what Luann had found herself in only the day before. Joaquin tightened his grip on the wheel and turned away from the arroyo, keeping the car from leaving the road, but the move cost him and the pickup was able to catch the back left fender of their vehicle. With another crunch, the cruiser shimmied to the left, turning into the center of the road with the truck actually forcing it along the asphalt. Joaquin again hit the accelerator and was finally able to pull away from the truck, but the driver was relentless and continued to loom directly behind them.

A shot suddenly rang out, cracking the rear window of the squad car.

"Get down!" Joaquin shouted. He pulled out his own weapon but quickly had to drop the pistol in his lap and return his hands to the wheel as they came across yet another turn in the road. It was all he could do to keep the car on the pavement and a few feet ahead of the aggressive driver behind them.

Another shot rang out and Joaquin heard a large bang as his left rear tire blew. The cruiser tilted and slowed dramatically as they found themselves suddenly riding on the rim of the wheel. Sparks and dust flew around them and caught his eye in his rearview mirror. His heart was clenched as he realized that they were both now in very big trouble. He said a silent prayer as the truck slammed into them again, pushing them closer and closer to the ditch, scraping metal against metal. He tried to get a look at the driver, but all he could see was a dark baseball cap, pulled low and covering the driver's features. He looked for his service weapon, but it had fallen to the floor and he kicked with his left foot, trying to draw it closer.

Luann cried out in fear and he gave up on the gun and reached over and grabbed her hand, knowing that this act of comfort may very well be his last. His heart constricted as he realized he might never see his daughter again. He knew instinctively that he and Luann were mere seconds from death.

Sirens suddenly echoed in the background, and the sound grew louder very quickly, making it obvious that his deputies were on their way and getting closer by the second. The truck's driver suddenly stopped his onslaught, put the vehicle in Reverse, and backed quickly away so he could maneuver around Joaquin's squad car. As the pickup sped away, Joaquin tried to see the driver, but once again, he was unable to get a clear view of his face. He was sure he was male, and he appeared to have dark hair, but he could tell very little else about him. Joaquin glimpsed the license plate, but all he could see was bits of the yellow-and-red design, showing that it was a New Mexico plate. The numbers were completely covered in mud, as was the sticker that said when the registration had to be renewed.

Joaquin turned quickly to Luann, noticing that she was still gripping his hand. "Are you okay?"

She took a moment to answer, and when she did, her voice was tremulous. “I think so.”

“Take deep breaths,” he encouraged as the sound of sirens increased even more. He released her hand and grabbed the radio, letting his two deputies know that they were okay. He told them both to keep following the truck and which direction it had gone, then turned back to Luann. “Let’s just sit here a few minutes and catch our breath. My deputies are almost here and are going after the truck.”

She nodded and leaned back against the seat and closed her eyes. Her face was still pale, and he could tell it was costing her to keep calm and appear collected. “Should I just go home?” she finally asked. “This has to be related to my father’s disappearance. But I keep going back and forth, wondering if I should give up. I feel like I’m supposed to be here, searching for the truth, but someone out there clearly doesn’t want me to get any answers. I’m not sure the truth is worth our lives.”

Right as she finished speaking, the two deputies sped by, still in pursuit of the silver truck with their sirens blazing. Joaquin waited for the wail of the sirens to die down again, then responded. “I don’t really understand why all of this is happening, especially since this is such an old case and we haven’t even confirmed your dad was on that plane that crashed, but there are obviously pieces of the story that we’re missing. I’m not ready to give up. But, honestly, the choice is yours, not mine. I’ll support whatever decision you make.”

He watched her carefully and could almost see the steel in her spine tighten. His respect for her grew. She was one tough cookie, even if she didn’t realize it herself.

"I've come too far to give up now. I'm going to see this investigation through until I get some answers."

"Sounds like a plan," he confirmed. He blew out a breath and rubbed the sweat from his forehead, secured his weapon, and reached for his phone. "Hello, Gary? Yeah, this is Joaquin." He explained what happened and their current location. "Would you mind bringing your tow truck over? I need you to pick up the squad car. It's going to need a bit of repair." He grimaced. "It would also be great if you could give us a ride back to your shop. Looks like we're going to need that Camry sooner than we thought."

Once he had Gary's reply, he hung up and turned back to Luann. "Do you want to sit here until Gary arrives?"

"I'd rather get some air," she said softly.

Joaquin nodded, turned and gave Lobo a pat and a quick once-over to make sure the dog was okay, and then got out and circled the car. He whistled in amazement when he saw the damage to the back of his squad car, but they were alive, and the cruiser could be fixed or replaced. He opened the passenger door and helped Luann out, then let Lobo out as well. The husky quickly approached Luann and whimpered until she bent down and hugged him.

"Are you okay, Lobo?" she said as she rubbed the animal affectionately.

"Hey, that dog seems more concerned about you than he does me," he complained with a smile.

She gave the husky another pat, then stood. "I've never been much of a dog person, but Lobo is special. He's growing on me."

Joaquin put on his cowboy hat, then motioned away

from the car. “He’s good at winning people over, especially if there is food around. But look out. When he sheds, there is hair everywhere, and I mean everywhere—inside your house, all over your furniture, coating your washing machine, your dryer…” His radio crackled and he gave her a nod. “Excuse me.”

Luann could hear Joaquin’s conversation with his deputies, and her heart sank.

Once again, his deputies had lost the silver truck, and the sheriff hadn’t been able to get a tag number during their attack. It sounded like they still had no idea who was attacking her, and without knowing who, it was awfully hard to fathom the motive of the perpetrator. Another deputy, who had apparently been doing some research earlier in the day, chimed into the conversation. After a very thorough check that had started that morning after the first incident, he had discovered that no one in Del Norte, including Carlos Sanchez, owned a pickup of that make, model and color. He’d also found out that there were over a hundred of the same trucks registered in the Albuquerque metropolitan area. That wasn’t too surprising, since Albuquerque boasted over half a million residents. Luann believed the driver was the same man who’d shot at them after they’d left the newspaper office, but she had to admit, she hadn’t gotten a good look at his features either.

How many times was this guy going to try to kill her? What if he actually succeeded?

Worry and fear swamped her as she waited with Joaquin and Lobo for Gary to appear with his tow truck. Thankfully, Gary brought a friend with him who had followed in his own vehicle, and who offered them a ride back to the garage so they could pick up the Camry.

A few minutes after getting the car, they grabbed a takeout order of hamburgers and fries from the local restaurant, and Joaquin was once again driving them toward Catia's house. They talked about Luann giving up her mission and returning home, but somewhere along the way, her resolve quickened into concrete. She *was* going to find out what happened to her dad, no matter what. Someone was guarding a secret. Someone wanted her dead. She still didn't know how all of the pieces fit together, but with Joaquin's help, she was going to figure this out.

Catia's house was a small, simple adobe-style building with a corral on the side that held a pretty brown mare feeding at a bale of hay. Joaquin parked near the garage, and then he, Luann and Lobo went up to the porch. Joaquin knocked as he scanned the area, staying vigilant for any threats or problems, as they waited.

A moment or two later, a short, gray-haired woman opened the door and peered up at them through thick metal-framed glasses.

"Hello, Ms. Catia," Joaquin said with a smile. "How are you doing this afternoon?"

"Well, if it isn't the sheriff? What are you doing way out here in my part of the world?"

"We came to talk a bit. Do you mind if we sit on your porch with you for a few minutes?"

The older lady shook her head. "No need to stay out there in the cold. Come on in." She was wrapped in a warm woolen Navajo blanket and motioned with her arm for them to enter, revealing a beaded leather necklace that was worn but still attractive. Her steel-colored hair was braided down her back and went nearly past her hips. Luann thought she was beautiful and classically stylish, and the old lady reminded her of some of the artisans she had seen selling jewelry and other items at a recent art show she had attended.

The two entered the house while Lobo curled up on the porch. "I'd like to introduce you to Luann St. John. She and I were doing some research down at the library, and we came across a few articles you wrote about twenty years ago about a plane crash that happened on the side of the mountain east of here."

Catia looked Luann up and down, then motioned for them to go into her living room, which contained two large brown overstuffed couches. "I guess you'd better sit on down. I just put the kettle on a few minutes ago. Would you like some tea or cocoa?" She disappeared for a few minutes without waiting for an answer and then returned with a heavily laden tray and mugs. Soon they were eating cookies and sipping cups of hot cocoa with little marshmallows on top.

"We looked at several back issues, and saw your byline," Luann intoned.

"What's your interest?" Catia asked, biting into the sugar cookie she'd taken from the small dish on the coffee table.

"I'm trying to find out if my father was on that plane, and why someone would want to stop me from finding out the truth about that accident," Luann answered. She explained everything she knew about the case, and what had been happening since she'd arrived in Del Norte. Joaquin sat quietly beside her, listening to her tell the story but only contributing a bit here and there for clarification.

Finally, Catia finished off her cookie and sat back in her chair. "Well, I retired a long time ago. I'm not sure I can tell you anything new that wasn't already included in the article. After all, that was over twenty years ago."

"Well, can you tell us about the search and rescue events?" Joaquin asked. "That might be enough to get us started."

"Anything that you remember would be helpful," Luann added.

"The plane crashed late in the afternoon," Catia replied, leaning back in her chair. "We heard the sound clear into town, and a few saw the fireball up the mountain. I think everyone saw the smoke. Anyway, police from over in Albuquerque showed up to help with the search, and they brought in big lights to shine on the crash site. The problem was, the crash happened in a really remote area." She blew out a breath. "It was a horrible scene. It looked like the plane had kind of bounced along the mountainside, and bits of the plane were scattered over a pretty large area."

"Did they find the pilot's body right away?"

Catia nodded. "Yes, he was still strapped in his chair in the cockpit. He was dead of course. He probably died on impact, but it was hard to tell. They took his body over to the morgue in Albuquerque and did an autopsy, but I don't remember the findings. I'm sure there's a report on it filed with the NTSB that could give you more information."

"I've read the report," Luann replied. "It said the pilot died from natural causes. They think he had a heart attack while he was flying and crashed because he was unconscious, or at least unable to control the plane."

Catia shrugged. "Well, there you go."

"Was there anything found to suggest there was more than one body?" Luann asked.

"No, but it was a huge mess for such a small aircraft. It destroyed a lot of trees," Catia replied. "The plane was used for skydiving, and equipment, clothing and parts of the plane were all over the place. Even so, as far as I know, they didn't recover anything from the wreckage that pointed to someone else also dying in the crash. And I know they only found the one body. The fuselage was so damaged that if anyone else had been on board, they surely would have died as well and been found in the wreckage."

Joaquin leaned forward. "Did you ever hear anything strange about the accident?"

Catia tilted her head. "Well, now that you mention it, there was a rumor that someone had stashed some diamonds on the plane, but I didn't hear that story until a few months later."

Luann raised an eyebrow as her heart started pounding against her chest. "We didn't see anything about that in the newspaper anywhere."

"That's because it was just rumors. I don't even know who started the rumors, or where they came from. I couldn't print something unsubstantiated, so I just ignored it. I think it was pure foolishness, if you want to know the truth."

"Who shared the story about the diamonds?" Luann asked.

Catia's face showed a thoughtful expression as she took another sip of her cocoa. She rubbed her weathered cheek with aged fingers. "Fabio Rodriquez was one of the first responders. He's the one who told me about the diamonds."

TEN

"Did Fabio believe the rumor about the diamonds was true?" Luann asked.

"He sure did," Catia responded. "His eyes lit up every time he talked about it. He was convinced he was going to find them somewhere near the crash site. When that didn't happen, he expanded the search farther out so that it matched the trajectory the NTSB mapped out in their final report. It was like Fabio was searching for buried treasure. He spent quite a bit of time out there in the desert looking for them, but as far as I know, it was all just a waste of time. After all of those trips, he never found a thing."

"Was he out there by himself?" Joaquin asked.

Catia took a moment to consider and chose another cookie from the plate on the table. "No, he had someone else he was working with, but before you ask, I have no idea who it was." She held up her hand as if to preclude any argument. "He mentioned having a partner, but never said the name. And frankly, I never asked. I told you already, I thought the story was pure foolishness. Nevertheless, the two of them looked for the diamonds for years, and for all I know, the partner will keep looking, even now that Fabio is dead."

She leaned back, chewing thoughtfully. "I mean, if there had been diamonds on that plane, the authorities would have been searching for them, too, and the FBI or other law enforcement would have jumped in and gotten involved, but that never happened. And if Fabio had ever found the diamonds, if there were any there to start with, he would have ended up living a life of luxury somewhere, not working for the state and then retiring to that little cabin in the woods."

She took another bite of her cookie, her face contemplative and her brow creased. "Now that I think about it, I wonder if Fabio didn't just really enjoy riding his horse around in the mountains, spending time out there with God and nature. He might have used the search for the diamonds as an excuse, but to me, he just seemed like a guy who appreciated camping in the outdoors and spending time alone in the woods."

Luann's emotions were on a roller coaster. One minute, she was excited about Catia's comments. The connection between the diamonds and the plane seemed to solidify her own theories that her father had somehow been on that plane, or at a minimum, that the crash was somehow connected to her father's disappearance and the diamond theft in Las Cruces. There was just too much circumstantial evidence. But where had the rumors come from? Who else had drawn the connection between the stolen diamonds and the plane? Questions swirled in her mind and made her stomach twist. Had her father or the thief somehow survived the crash and carried the tale?

Was Fabio the thief? The thought nagged at her like a

splinter beneath the skin. He was the right age, that much was certain, but his features didn't quite match the blurred face she'd studied so many times on the surveillance tape. Fabio's jawline was sharper, his hair darker.

Still, she couldn't dismiss him. That video had been awful—grainy, distorted, the shadows swallowing more than they revealed. The perpetrator's movements had been jerky, almost unnatural, as if he knew the camera was there and had been deliberately trying to mask his appearance. Different hair, a false beard, maybe even platform shoes…any disguise could have hidden the truth.

Luann's pulse quickened as the uncertainties roiled. What if she had been chasing a ghost all this time, a phantom carefully constructed to mislead? And who was this partner? Had Fabio's partner killed him?

Was this mystery man someone still here in Del Norte—someone she had already spoken to? Was someone out there even now, laughing with neighbors, living life, all the while hiding behind a carefully constructed mask? Could he be walking the same streets, earning trust with every easy word, every casual wave, while carrying the weight of murder and robbery in his past, a truth buried deep in the dark?

The thought chilled Luann to the bone. Faces she had encountered over the past few days flickered through her mind—shopkeepers, ranch hands, even men she had once considered harmless. Any one of them could have been the wolf in sheep's clothing, blending so seamlessly into the fabric of the town that no one thought to look closer.

Her stomach twisted. Had she sat across from him already, her pen scratching notes while he lied with a straight face? Had she smiled politely, thanked him for his time, never realizing she was in the presence of a killer?

A prickle of unease climbed her spine. In Del Norte, trust was currency—neighbors watched over one another, cared for each other. If that bond had been betrayed, if a murderer had been hiding in plain sight all these years, then no one—not even she—was truly safe.

Good grief. Would the questions ever end, or was she destined to circle this mystery forever, caught in the thief's shadow?

"You know," Catia said as she waved her hand and broke into Luann's thoughts. "You aren't the first one to come asking about that crash."

Joaquin's face registered his surprise and he leaned forward. "Who else came calling?"

"There was another man who stopped by a couple of days ago," Catia admitted. "He also said he'd heard there were diamonds on that plane and wanted to know if anyone had ever found them."

"What did he look like?" Luann asked.

"Tall, muscular guy. Kind of looked like a private investigator—at least the ones I've seen on television. Dark hair, dark eyes. Well dressed in a chamois shirt and khakis."

"Do you remember what he was driving?"

"I didn't look to see what kind of car he had," Catia admitted. "It sure is strange that there's suddenly all of this interest in finding out about something that happened so long ago. I mean it's been twenty years! What's going on?"

"I was wondering the same thing," Luann answered. "For me, I can only say that since my mother's illness is progressing so quickly, I'm motivated to find the answers before it's too late. I want to know if my father was on that plane."

Luann was wondering if Joaquin thought the man Catia described matched the shooter who had been following and taking shots at her, but she couldn't tell anything by looking at his expressionless face. If that gunman wasn't responsible for the attacks, what did that mean? Were others also interested in recovering the diamonds and racing to solve the mystery? Why now?

To her, the diamonds didn't even matter. All she wanted to discover was what had happened to her father. The insurance company had paid the claim years ago, so at this point, she assumed that if the diamonds were ever recovered, they would go to the insurance company to reimburse it for the payout they'd had to make to the store owner. Sure, the stones were valuable. But they weren't hers.

Luann and Joaquin thanked Catia for her time and then headed back to the car. Luann met Joaquin's eyes once they were seated in the Camry with Lobo once again enjoying the back seat. "Well, at least some of the pieces are falling into place. It looks like someone besides me believes those diamonds were on the plane."

"You're right," Joaquin agreed. "When we were in Fabio's cabin, I saw a grid map of the area east of here." He pulled out his phone and showed her the picture he'd taken. "I wasn't sure if the map had anything to do with your search or not, but now I think there's definitely a connection. I would imagine that if we checked the NTSB report, we'd see that the map of the crash site matches the zone that Fabio was searching. Catia said it covered a pretty large region. See these three areas? It's like he'd already searched these other parts but hadn't made it to these yet." He pointed to the three sections without an X. "It's no wonder he saved these three sections for last. They're in a very difficult stretch of mountain to get to and are pretty far away from the actual crash site."

"Are there any roads that go up to that area?"

"Nope," Joaquin responded. "I think the only way in is by horseback. It's way too far to walk, and the terrain makes it unsuitable for ATVs. And at least with horses, you can pack in the supplies you need and make the trip more manageable." The car was already getting a bit chilly, and he started the engine and got the heat going.

Luann thought about the situation for a moment, waiting for the heater to start blowing warmer air. Once it did, she rubbed her hands in front of the vent. "I have a map that shows the debris field from the NTSB report. It's in my room at the bed-and-breakfast. If you're right, it sounds like my next move is to go out the crash site myself and do some looking around. Then, if we don't find any clues, the next move would be to search these three grids."

"What do you think you'll find at the crash site after twenty years?"

"Probably nothing," Luann said with a shrug. "But someone doesn't want me here, so there must be a reason, and that sounds like a reasonable place to start. All I can do is keep searching until I get as many answers as I can. If nothing else, maybe seeing the crash site will give me some closure so I can move on with my life without wondering about the past."

Joaquin put the car in Reverse, pulled out of Catia's

driveway, and headed back to Del Norte. "Well, I guess that's our next step then."

"*Our* next step?" Luann was delighted that he was considering going on the trip with her, but surely he had other duties to perform besides keeping her safe. She'd probably have to hire a guide, and maybe even a bodyguard, but she didn't think it was fair to keep monopolizing the sheriff's time. Hopefully, whoever had been trying to kill her wouldn't be motivated to follow her on a horseback-riding trip out into the woods.

Joaquin adjusted his cowboy hat and met her eyes again. "Yes. *Our* next step." He turned his eyes back to the road. "If you think I'm going to send you out into the wilderness by yourself, especially with all of the danger you've faced lately, you're crazy."

"But you have a daughter. She needs you in town."

"Camila is used to my schedule, and I have a great support system in place. Don't worry. I can make appropriate arrangements for her."

Luann nodded, though a trace of guilt still tugged at her. Part of her worried about taking Joaquin away from his daughter, pulling him into her quest when his world already carried its own weight. But he was a grown man—steady, deliberate—and fully capable of deciding where his responsibilities began and ended. And he had chosen to be here. With her. If he was determined to ride with her out to the crash site, there was little she could do to dissuade him. And, actually, she didn't even want to try. The truth was, she felt safer when he was close, his quiet strength wrapping around her like an unseen shield. Even the simple cadence of his voice steadied her frayed nerves.

She was surprised by her feelings and found herself

enjoying his company more than she'd expected, his wry humor sneaking past her defenses, the warmth in his gaze stirring something inside her she had never felt before. The thought of spending days with him—side by side on horseback, nights beneath the stars—both thrilled and unsettled her. She knew almost nothing about riding or camping in the desert, but she was determined to learn. And with Joaquin at her side, she wasn't afraid to try.

Joaquin kept his eyes on the road, but his attention kept straying to Luann. She sat only a few feet away, determination shining in her eyes. He admired that about her—how she dove into things that scared her and refused to let fear dictate her path. Most people would have walked away from a mission like hers long ago, but not Luann. That same fire drew him in, no matter how much he tried to resist it. He told himself he was there to keep her safe, to see her through her desert quest and back again. But the truth was harder to ignore each passing day—he wanted to be near her, wanted to be the one she leaned on when the road grew dangerous, the one she trusted in both her fear and her hope. Now he just had to figure out what, if anything, he was going to do about it.

Once they were back in Del Norte, they spent the next hour or so perusing Luann's computer. The National Transportation Safety Board's investigation report filled the screen—pages of technical language, diagrams and stark black-and-white photographs that seemed to leach warmth from the room. Joaquin scrolled through each page, his eyes intent, his jaw tightening at certain details. He finally leaned back, the laptop's glow fading as he pushed it aside, but the images and words still burned in his mind. The report raised more questions than it answered, and that unsettled him. Yet, even as his thoughts circled the wreckage and the investigation, he found his attention drifting to Luann. She was sitting so close that a strand of her hair brushed his arm, carrying the faint scent of lavender and desert air.

She was waiting for his reaction, her eyes searching his face with a mixture of hope and dread. The vulnerability there struck him harder than the grim photos ever could. She was braver than she realized, chasing answers that might very well shatter her, and he couldn't let her face that alone. Protecting her had become more than duty—it was instinct, bone-deep and unshakable. His chest tightened as he realized how much he wanted to be the one she turned to, not just for safety, but for comfort, for trust. And that want was dangerous, because with every hour they spent together, walking this razor's edge of secrets and danger, his resolve to keep a careful distance was unraveling fast.

"I'm sure you realize that the authorities only listed one fatality, the pilot, in the final report. There's no mention of anyone else on board, and no proof that anyone else was even involved with the flight."

"I'm aware," Luann answered. "They never found my father's body. I'm thinking that if he was on that plane, along with the criminal who stole the diamonds, the two of them bailed out somewhere along the way. It was a plane designed for skydiving."

Joaquin blew out a breath. "If that happened, it could have occurred anytime along the plane's flight. You're talking about hundreds of miles to search. And even if we conducted that search, we'd probably never find his body."

"I understand," Luann said quietly. "But I have to try. I know this is like looking for a needle in a haystack. Even if we find absolutely nothing at all, I still have to go up there on that mountain and see the crash site."

Joaquin studied her for moment, lost in thought. Before he could say another word, she took her computer and navigated back to the pages in the report that showed the photos.

"Although the plane wreckage was removed long ago and taken to a storage facility by the authorities, I'd like for you to take a look at these pictures." She clicked on the first of the bunch so that it filled the screen. "There are several that show the outside of the plane, but this one shows the inside of the fuselage."

Joaquin leaned closer, examining the photo, and used the mouse to enlarge parts of the image to get a better look. He noticed some markings on the wall that seemed out of place, and tried to make that section of the photo even bigger on the screen so he could figure out exactly what he was looking at. At first the design was a bit blurry, but with a few clicks, he was able to sharpen the focus. "What's that?" he asked, pointing at the design.

Luann frowned, then leaned even closer to the screen. Suddenly excitement lit her eyes and she gasped. "I can't believe I missed that! I think my father must have drawn that sketch!" She took the mouse and moved the photo a couple of different ways, examining the drawing. . "Look at the right bottom corner! Doesn't that look like the letters 'HSJ'?"

Joaquin nodded. "Looks like that to me."

Luann adjusted the photo again, a smile on her face. "My father liked to doodle, and he would always sign things with his initials, HSJ, Henry St. John, like in this picture. See the little twirl at the top of the 'H'?"

Joaquin took another look. The crude design was small, and seemed to depict a man and an open parachute by the door to the plane but it was incomplete, and could have been interpreted a number of different ways. He leaned closer. Could the drawing have been made with some sort of permanent marker? He fiddled with the computer some, but wasn't able to improve the photo enough to glean anything further. He wished there was more to the artwork, but the initials alone were a telling clue. If those were Luann's father's initials, then he had definitely been on that plane.

Luann smiled and a light shone in her eyes that made her entire countenance glow. It was clear that she also understood the implications of finding the artwork, regardless of the meaning behind the figures in the drawing. "I'm so glad you noticed that design. I bet my father was trying to tell us something, but didn't get a chance to finish it since the plane was going down, or something else happened that stopped him."

Joaquin nodded. "That's an excellent theory."

Luann tapped her chin with her finger and tilted her head slightly to the left. "I'm also starting to wonder if Fabio was the thief who robbed the jewelry store and forced my dad onto that plane."

Joaquin was silent again. Finally, he ran his hands through his hair. "I guess it's possible. We'll have to do some research to see if we can discover Fabio's whereabouts twenty years ago to either support or refute that theory." He pushed his hat back on his head. "Look, I'm going with you tomorrow, no matter what. I just don't want you to be too disappointed if we don't find anything, one way or the other. It's been twenty years, after all. I'm not sure we're going to find anything of value. I can pretty much guarantee that if there were diamonds on that plane, the authorities would have found them already when they analyzed the crash site."

Luann settled back, and he saw relief in her eyes. He had no doubt she would go with a guide if he wasn't available, but he wanted to be the one to go with her. It was his duty to protect her. It was as simple as that.

"I know. I get it, and I really don't care about the diamonds." She drew her lips into a thin line. "There's some piece of this puzzle we're missing though. And Fabio is dead. So, if he was the thief all those years ago, why was he killed? And who is the mystery partner?"

"Agreed. I have no idea what we're missing."

They spread the evidence out before them—the NTSB map with the plane's probable trajectory, the photo of the marked-up map Joaquin had taken at Fabio's cabin and printed at his office and a worn paper map from the glove box of Joaquin's cruiser. Side by side, the patterns told a story neither of them wanted to admit. Fabio's marks clustered around the crash site first, a spider's web of lines and circles, as if he had scoured every inch of ground. Then the lines stretched outward, tracing the path the plane had taken before it went down.

Joaquin's gut tightened. This wasn't casual curiosity. Fabio had been methodical, relentless. A man didn't chase ghosts for years unless he believed something worth finding was still out there.

Luann leaned closer, her fingertip brushing the paper map as she traced one of Fabio's large red X's that marked off one of the grid squares. Her voice was low, tight with emotion. "It's almost like he knows something the investigators missed—some clue my father might have left behind." Her words hung in the air, sharp as broken glass. Joaquin watched the determination in her face, but beneath it he caught a flicker of fear. And he couldn't shake the chill crawling up his own spine. Whatever Fabio had been searching for, people had already killed to keep buried.

Would they be able to solve this mystery before the murderer tried again to take her life?

ELEVEN

With a couple of phone calls, Joaquin was able to make reservations with Levi Sanchez, the rancher who ran a wilderness excursion business east of Del Norte, to rent a couple of horses and a horse trailer for a ride out to the crash site. Levi was also Carlos Sanchez's father, and Joaquin was a bit nervous about doing business with him in case Carlos was actually connected to the investigation. But they really didn't have a choice. Levi's ranch was the only place nearby where they could rent the horses and equipment they needed for their trip to the crash site, and in this case, location mattered and would make the trip infinitely easier.

Once that was set, the two took Luann's Camry over to a wilderness store in Tijeras so Luann could buy some warmer clothing for the trip since the temperature had dipped lower than she'd expected. They didn't plan to stay out overnight, so they didn't need much, but it always paid to be prepared, and Luann decided a nice thermal undershirt would really help. Joaquin decided to buy a new pair of gloves as long as they were there and picked out a warm pair that were oversized and easier on his hands. He needed a looser fit due to his burns, and Luann picked up the bill to thank him for all of his assistance, despite his objections.

On the trip back to Del Norte, Joaquin used his phone to make arrangements for Camila's care during the next day. Susanna was eager to help, and agreed to take the little girl to preschool, and watch her in the afternoon and evening in case Luann and Joaquin were late returning.

He got Luann back to the bed-and-breakfast right before dinner, and they had a pleasant evening, just talking and playing charades with Susanna, her husband and Camila until they all turned in for the night. Joaquin checked Luann's room to make sure she was safe, and once again verified every window and door was locked tightly. He hadn't seen any other threat since the silver truck had driven away that afternoon, but his deputies had spent several hours researching a variety of leads without any real success. The bottom line was that they still didn't know where the threat against Luann was coming from, or how involved Fabio had been in past events.

He paused a moment outside her locked door, thinking through the events of the evening. He and Camila had spent several nights with Susanna and Ted and loved the older couple like family. But he had to admit, Luann had been a welcome addition to their evening activities, and he had truly enjoyed watching her interact with Camila. The child had immediately taken to Luann's smile and friendly demeanor, and had spent most of the evening on Luann's lap, whispering secrets into her ear and putting stickers in a Bible story booklet she had gotten in preschool that day. Luann seemed to love children, and Joaquin had been content to just relax and watch the two of them together. It warmed his heart.

What was he going to do when this case was over and Luann returned home to Clovis? The thought bothered him more than he wanted to admit, and he chewed on it for the next hour as sleep eluded him. Even though it had only been a couple of days, he was finding it hard to imagine life without her.

Was it possible to start caring about someone so soon after meeting them? He finally got to sleep, but it wasn't easy. His heart felt like it was finally beating for the first time in two years.

Early the next morning, the two headed out early to Levi's ranch, refreshed and ready to see what they could discover.

Levi was already outside when they arrived, working near the barn, and thankfully, there was no sign of Carlos. The older man ambled out to their car and met them right as they were getting out of the Camry. He was tall and solidly built, with leathery, weathered skin and an easy smile. He was dressed in jeans and a sheepskin coat and had on a tan Stetson with a nice silver band.

"I heard you're investigating that old plane crash that happened a long time ago," he said with no preamble whatsoever. His smile turned into a frown, and his eyes narrowed as he spoke. "Are you sure this is a good idea? I doubt you'll find anything new after all of this time, and it won't be a comfortable ride. The trails back there have long since disappeared, too. If you're going out on a trail ride, I suggest you try something near the East Pass. That would be a much better experience for you both."

Joaquin frowned, surprised by the older man's attitude. He'd had to deal with Levi several times over the years due to his son's criminal behavior, but Levi had always seemed like a caring man than was invested in his community. His current body language and attitude surprised Joaquin. Did the older man have something to hide? Joaquin wasn't sure what to think, but an uneasiness settled in his stomach.

A cool wind blew through the area and Joaquin's focus shifted to Luann as she shivered and rubbed her arms. He wondered if she was really cold or just turned off by the less than friendly greeting they'd received. Or maybe she was picking up on the negative vibes that Levi seemed to be putting off? Joaquin moved in front of Luann as if to shield her from the older man's pessimistic attitude, and Lobo also ambled over and stood by his side, as if the dog also felt like Luann needed protection.

"We're sure about our plans," Joaquin answered. "I've got a map and the weather is crisp and cold. It should be a nice day for riding." He put on his own brown Stetson. "Did you live up here when the crash happened? I can't remember when you bought your ranch here in Del Norte."

"It was before my time, but I heard about it. I bought this ranch a couple of years later, if I remember right."

"Well, like I said, we've got a map, and since you live up this way, I was hoping to go over it with you to make sure I'm parking in the best spot. We want to get as close as possible by truck before we get on the horses."

"Like I said, it's a difficult journey," Levi warned. "The horses might struggle with the terrain."

"I've been around horses all my life," Joaquin responded. "I promise we'll take good care of your animals."

"I know you will," Levi admitted, his hands on his hips. "But I'm just saying—it's a rough trip, especially for a city girl." He motioned to Luann. "She doesn't look like she's used to riding horses."

Luann's eyes narrowed, but Joaquin spoke up before she could comment. "She'll do fine, and I'll be there to help if we have any difficulties."

"Well, I can tell I'm not going to talk you out of it," Levi said with a shake of his head, "so I'll rent you the horses and a truck and trailer that will work perfectly for what you're trying to do." He motioned toward the barn where an older ranch hand was standing by the door, and the man nodded and disappeared. Joaquin thought it was Kenny Garcia but only got a short glimpse of him before Levi was speaking again. "Can I see your map?"

Joaquin nodded. "I bought a paper map since I doubt there's cell service out there and we probably won't be able to use the maps on our phones. We're trying to get as close as possible to the crash site." He pulled the folded map out of his pocket, opened it and showed Levi where they were headed. The older man didn't seem surprised by their goal but showed them the best road to take.

"Here's the easiest route and the closest spot where you can park the truck," Levi said, pointing to a section on the map. "I heard they created a road of sorts twenty years ago just so they could access the crash site, but once they recovered the parts of the plane they were interested in, the road never got used again. It's probably pretty overgrown by now. I haven't been up there myself in years."

Joaquin marked it, but suddenly he felt a cold chill sweep up his spine.

Was somebody watching them?

He glanced at Luann, who had a strange look on her face, as if she'd also sensed that someone had them under surveillance. She took a step closer to him and reached down and rubbed Lobo on the head as if reassuring herself that they were safe.

The uneasy feeling didn't dissipate. If anything, it grew stronger. He looked over at the barn, but didn't see any sign of Kenny Garcia or anyone else. "Why don't we go into the barn?" Joaquin asked, hoping that the structure could offer them a measure of safety if there truly was someone out there keeping an eye on them. Without waiting for a response, he grabbed Luann's hand and quickly pulled her through the large open doors and past the first few stalls.

"Is everything okay?" Luann asked softly for Joaquin's ears alone.

"I'm not sure. I just got an uneasy feeling and thought we should talk here instead of out in the open."

"Good call," Luann agreed. "Even Lobo was acting like something wasn't quite right."

Joaquin looked down at his dog and noticed that the animal was on high alert, with his ears perked up and the hair on his back raised in awareness.

Levi was slow to follow them but eventually came into the barn. "You two okay?" he asked. "You're acting a little squirrelly."

"Someone has been taking shots at Luann, so we came in here in an abundance of caution," Joaquin said tightly. "Have you seen Carlos lately?"

Levi narrowed his eyes. "He went into town a little while ago. He needed to pick up some feed." He took a step forward. "You're not suggesting my son was taking shots at this lady, are you?"

Joaquin put up his hands. "I'm not suggesting anything.

I was just wondering how he was doing. He was pretty upset about Fabio's death the other day and I wanted to check on him." He motioned toward the stalls where several horses were housed. "Which horses should we take?"

They heard a sound behind them, and the two turned to see Kenny Garcia storing some tack in a nearby storage closet.

"Hey, Mr. Garcia," Joaquin called. The man had worked for Levi for as long as Joaquin could remember. He was single and had no children, and while he had once been a regular at the local diner, Joaquin rarely saw him come into town anymore. He usually kept to himself, and while Joaquin had heard stories from the previous sheriff about the man's wilder, younger years, he'd never really had many opportunities to talk to him. Joaquin guessed that Garcia was now in his early sixties, and had a thick head of snowy-white hair, a bushy mustache and large, powerful arms from all of the manual labor he'd done over the last several years. He was tall and usually sported an off-white straw cowboy hat. Rumor had it that Garcia had once ridden bulls on the rodeo circuit, but Joaquin had never seen him perform. The older man waved and started polishing a saddle with a soft cloth.

"Hey, yourself," Garcia answered. "Heading out for a trail ride?"

"We are," Joaquin confirmed. "How have you been? It's been ages since I've seen you."

"Doin' fine," Garcia answered. He finished with the saddle and brought it over to the trailer that was parked near the entrance to the barn. "We'll have you outfitted here in a bit. This saddle is the last thing I wanted to add before we got the horses loaded." He smiled but seemed distracted and didn't look Joaquin in the eye, which the sheriff thought was a little strange. He shrugged it off though. Right now, he was suspicious of everyone and was admittedly on high alert since he'd felt the strange sensation of being watched only moments before.

A few minutes later, Levi and Kenny had trailered two horses, and Joaquin and Luann were on their way. They left the Camry at Levi's barn, and Joaquin drove the rented truck from the ranch and followed the map toward the trailhead. It took them a good hour to arrive at the designated location, but Joaquin wasn't surprised. They hadn't gone that far, but there wasn't much of a road, and the trip had been slow as they'd picked their way along the rocky terrain. Finally, there was no more road to follow, and Joaquin parked. They got the horses out and saddled them, and then made sure they had water and snacks packed before heading out.

Luann was mounted on a small bay gelding, and Joaquin was riding a larger, black gelding with a small white star on his forehead. Both were beautiful animals and seemed to be well-mannered. Lobo followed behind the animals, and the small group slowly headed away from the road and into the wilderness.

The crash site was on the eastern side of the Sandia Mountains, and the terrain was difficult, just as Levi had predicted. Although some of the land was flat at the beginning, they soon found themselves going mostly uphill and around large boulders of granite. A variety of trees, from junipers and firs to ponderosa pines, filled the landscape. Now that they were mounted and walking through the trees, the feelings of danger had subsided somewhat, and Joaquin found himself finally relaxing a bit and enjoying the journey. He was outdoors in New Mexico, the sky was a cloudless clear blue, and he was riding through beautiful country with a lovely woman at his side. He said a prayer of thankfulness, acknowledging that God was good, and had been protecting both of them during the travails of the last few days.

"Good thing we brought some snacks, just in case. This is pretty slow going," Luann quipped a couple of hours later as they passed under another stand of large pines. She pulled out a granola bar and offered him one as well. He shook his head and she stowed his back in her pocket, then took a bite of her own.

Joaquin reined in his horse and took a moment to just study the area around him, then pulled out the map from his jacket pocket. "It looks like we're pretty close to the crash site." He looked up again and pointed toward a clearing in the distance. "See that area over there? That's where we're headed."

He tucked the map away again and Luann nudged her horse to follow his. A sense of foreboding swept over her as they approached. She had been wanting to come to the crash site for so long that it was hard to believe she was actually there, on the precipice of realizing her hopes. Even if she didn't discover the ultimate fate of her father, after visiting the crash site she would be one step closer to putting the entire situation behind her, at least in her mind.

They arrived at the spot a few minutes later, and Luann was only vaguely able to recognize the landmarks from the crash report photos. Trees and other vegetation had reestablished themselves, obscuring the majority of the crash site. She dismounted and tied her horse's lead rope to a sapling, and behind her, she heard Joaquin do the same.

The larger pieces of the plane had all been removed, but even though the crash had happened twenty years ago, Luann was still able to find, mixed with the dirt and gravel, tiny bits of plastic and rubber that had undoubtedly at one time been part of the plane. The pieces were degraded from spending so much time in the New Mexico sun, but they were in better shape than the bits of metal she found that were corroded and rusted. A small section of land was just dirt with no vegetation, and Luann imagined that the soil had been contaminated with spilled fuels and lubricants, keeping plants from growing over the area even after twenty years had passed.

A heaviness filled her heart as she looked over the landscape. Had this been her father's last sight before he died? She knew it had been a long shot that she would see or find anything from the crash site that would bring her the peace she was searching for, but she still walked the area for a good amount of time, just looking around and picking up and examining whatever she found that didn't seem to naturally belong. After an hour or so, she sat on a boulder and examined the pile of things she'd found. Nothing was even really identifiable—she could tell the bits were parts of the plane only because she knew the history of what had happened in the vicinity, but they gave her no clues whatsoever about her father's disappearance.

But what had she expected? The NTSB had taken the fuselage and every other possible item for their investigation, and they were the experts.

She was just an English teacher from Clovis who had

loved her father. She couldn't even prove that he'd been on the plane. Was she just looking for a needle in a haystack?

Joaquin had stayed out of her way and to the side of the clearing, letting her peruse the area alone, but when she was finished, he joined her by the boulder. "Did you find what you were looking for?"

"Yes," she replied, "and no." She sighed. "I didn't really expect to find much. It's just really sad to think of my father dying here, in this desolate area, being totally alone." She tossed a rock across the field. "And what's worse is that I don't even know for sure if he was on that plane, or if he's even dead! I mean, I think he drew that drawing on the fuselage wall, but I don't have any real proof. And if that was him, where is he? Why hasn't anybody found his body? This whole thing is so frustrating. I want closure so I can move on with my life, and I'm not even sure if I'm on the right path to finding it. So far, after all that's happened in Del Norte, all I have is more questions."

"I'm sorry you didn't find what you were looking for," Joaquin responded quietly. "I've learned the hard way that sometimes it's impossible to get the answers."

There was a wistful tone to his voice and Luann studied him for a moment. A flash of pain crossed his features, and her own pain was momentarily forgotten as she sought a way to lessen his. "Do you mean your ex-wife?"

Joaquin tilted his head. "Yes. Sorry, I don't mean to compare our situations."

"Don't be silly," Luann replied. "You can talk to me about anything. I promise, I won't judge."

Joaquin paused a moment as if considering her words, then finally shrugged. "Looking back, I can understand why she left me. I mean, I'm no prince, and I work long hours, but I'll never understand why she left our sweet daughter." He pushed his cowboy hat further back on his head. "I mean, don't get me wrong—I'm glad she didn't fight me for custody and we don't have to ping-pong her back and forth between homes as she's growing up, but I think not having a mom is going to impact Camila in a lot of different ways that I haven't even thought about yet."

"Don't sell yourself short," Luann said with a smile and a friendly nudge. "She was foolish to leave you both." She tilted her head. "And I wouldn't worry about Camila. I've already seen how your town pulls together to help her out. She's going to benefit from all of those special relationships, like with Susanna and Ted. Kids are resilient, and Camila seems strong and confident. I really think she's going to be okay."

Their eyes met, and Luann sucked in a breath as a gentle warmth of attraction bloomed between them. It was an unexpected sensation, and although she meant what she'd said about his ex's departure, she was also surprised at her own forwardness. She wasn't looking for a relationship and would be leaving Del Norte in a matter of days. Still, she couldn't deny that she was attracted to the sheriff. Joaquin was a gentle giant—a caring man who had already gone way beyond the expected to help and protect her. She hadn't spent much time with Camila, but she seemed like a sweet little girl with a big heart. Luann couldn't control the other woman's behavior, but maybe she could help heal some of the destruction the woman had left behind.

She was about to say something more that she hoped would encourage him when she heard a sound behind her. She whirled around but saw nothing out of the ordinary. Had Lobo bumped a rock that had shifted? Her eyes quickly searched the area, but even Lobo was on full alert, the hair on his back standing on end.

She turned back to Joaquin who had his hand on the butt of his gun, ready. He, too, must have heard the sound. An uneasy feeling swept over her as she motioned to the horses. "Maybe it's time we headed back?"

"Sure thing," he said out loud. Then, in a softer voice for her ears only he said, "We may not be alone out here. Keep your eyes open, and let's get back to the horses."

"I'm done," she said in a regular voice, and she started walking toward the horses. Uneasiness swept up her spine and her heart started beating like a bass drum in her chest. She felt the same uneasiness she'd experienced outside the barn when they'd first arrived at Levi's ranch. Who would have followed them out here? Was Carlos still a threat, and following them, or was someone else out there, watching them?

And who wanted her dead?

TWELVE

They weren't alone.

Joaquin studied the area as the fine hairs of his neck rose to attention. He didn't know who was out there, but somebody had followed them into the wilderness. He pushed aside the emotions that were swirling in his chest and focused on what he was good at—his job. He hadn't seen anyone lurking in the shadows, but Lobo's behavior bolstered his own feelings of uneasiness. There was definitely someone out there hiding in the desert, watching them.

They mounted up and started heading back, all three of them on alert as they kept their eyes open, constantly scanning the area.

Suddenly, Lobo started barking and growling, obviously upset by something that was in front of them and behind a large outcrop of rocks. The wind blew, making the tree branches hum and sway as they scratched against each other. Unlike Lobo, Joaquin didn't hear anything that revealed the person who was out there, but he could just make out the blue denim of a sleeve as it retreated behind the granite.

He pulled his weapon and motioned for Luann to stop

her horse. "I know you're there," Joaquin called. "I'm armed, and I'm the sheriff. Now come out slowly with your hands up."

The next thing he saw was the barrel of a rifle being brought down on them. He fired once to give them cover, shouting over his shoulder at Luann while he motioned with his arm, "Head toward the trees!" He fired again, making sure Luann and her horse were safely ensconced among the nearby tree trunks as he spurred his own horse to follow her at a gallop. Then he turned and fired a third time toward the rocks as he entered the tree line.

A bullet hit a ponderosa pine near his left shoulder, sending bark and bits of wood into the air. Joaquin ducked and kept moving. He couldn't gallop here because the trees were so close together, but he was still moving at a pretty fast clip. Luann was about thirty feet ahead of him, bending low in the saddle. She chanced a look behind her and their eyes met. He saw fear there, but also a determination that bolstered his own resolve. "I'm good," he yelled. "Don't stop." They zigzagged through the stand of trees and came to a flatter area just as another shot rang out. The horse Luann was riding startled and jerked to the right. Luann grabbed the horn of her saddle, righting herself as the gelding continued to gallop up toward another group of pines at breakneck speed. Joaquin let out a breath of relief as she got her seat back. It wasn't easy to stay mounted on a scared horse galloping through unfamiliar territory, especially when she wasn't an experienced equestrian.

They continued galloping across the valley and then started up the other side into a rocky area. Two more shots rang out, but they came from farther south. Joaquin gritted his teeth. He didn't think the change meant there were two shooters out there. Instead, he was pretty sure the rifleman had just moved and was now shooting at them from a new location. He also had to be on horseback. There was no way he had run that far on foot in the small amount of time it had taken him to relocate. Unfortunately, the new spot the bullets were coming from was closer to their current trajectory, and Luann was in more danger now than she had been five minutes ago.

Joaquin's chest felt heavy as adrenaline pumped through him. He couldn't lose Luann. He hadn't known her long, but what he knew, he liked. It was his job to keep her safe, but the feelings he was starting to experience in her presence went further than job-related obligation. He fired once again in the general direction of where the bullets were coming from, hoping to give Luann a bit more cover as they raced for their lives. Mentally, he did the math as he rode, counting how many bullets he had left in his weapon and the spare mag he kept in his belt. He had to be conservative with his shots if they were going to survive.

The horses started up the rocky incline, scrambling to gain purchase on the slippery terrain. They had to slow considerably, and Joaquin was able to catch up with Luann about midway up the hill as they continued climbing side by side. She cried out as her horse stumbled, and he reached over and helped her stay in the saddle as the bay gelding struggled with the slope. They made it to the top, then headed for cover behind a group of piñons.

Once behind the trees, they reined in their horses and paused a moment to catch their breath. "I want you to keep going west," Joaquin said tightly. "I'm going to circle around behind the shooter so I can stop him."

She took a deep breath and studied her hands for a moment, then looked up again. "Okay. I think I can find my way back to the truck. Do you want to meet up there?" Her eyes were large, and he could read the anxiety, but she also appeared to be getting stronger and more resolute as she faced each challenge, and his respect for her went up another notch. He knew from experience that it was amazingly difficult to be terrified and still do what needed to be done. Gone was the doubt and the hesitation in her face. He could tell by her demeanor and body language that she was now prepared to do whatever was necessary to survive and see this situation through to the very end.

"No, I don't want you to wait for me," Joaquin said forcefully. He handed her the keys. "These are for the truck. As soon as you get there, you drive away and get as far away from here as possible. Don't even take the time to load up your horse. Just tie him up to a tree and get out of Dodge. We'll come back for him later once this mess is over."

"I won't leave you behind," she said vehemently.

"Yes, you will." He scowled. "I know this country. I can make it out on foot if I have to. You get the truck and head straight back to my office. Don't go to Levi's ranch. Just find Ricky or the other deputy and let them know what happened. They can come look for me if I haven't checked in by the time you get to Del Norte."

Luann frowned and narrowed her eyes. "You're not hearing me. I don't want to leave you behind!"

"I heard you. I just don't agree. Look, I'm the sheriff.

I'm trained for situations like this. Please, just do what I'm telling you. I'll meet you back at my office." He lowered his head and moved so close that he could see the flecks of gray in her eyes. "I promise." He wanted to say more—something else to reassure her—but nothing came to mind as the urge to protect her became almost overwhelming. She had to survive and be safe. He would give his life for her. He knew it the moment he looked into her eyes.

"You can't promise that," she replied softly as her horse shifted beneath her.

"I promise to do my best, and not to put myself into any unnecessary danger."

She considered his compromise, but he could tell she still wasn't happy, even as she capitulated. "I'm going, but only so I can get help. I'll come back for you." There was a fierceness in her tone that warmed him despite the chill in the air. She pulled on the reins, nudged her horse, and was soon galloping away from him.

Joaquin turned his own horse, his reins in one hand and his weapon in the other as he circled behind the trees, then moved up the hill, hoping his path wasn't visible to the shooter. He backtracked, making his best guess as to the criminal's location. He didn't like sending Luann off alone, but didn't see any other option. Catching the killer was imperative. The man had already tried to kill her several times, and he had to be stopped before he actually succeeded.

It was going to end today.

He pushed his horse harder, trying to move faster to catch the killer.

Another bullet suddenly flew by Luann's head and she ducked, trying to stay on her horse and out of the shooter's sights. Apparently, the gunman had guessed her new trajectory and had adjusted accordingly. She called out encouragement to her gelding as he raced across an open field between two valleys, knowing she was once again running for her life. She was filled with a host of emotions, from downright terror to frustration and confusion. Nothing that was happening made any sense.

She pulled on her reins and turned her horse, trying to make herself into a more difficult target as she dodged the sagebrush and cacti. She didn't know much about escaping from an unhinged man with a gun, but she was hoping that her route was making it at least a little challenging for the shooter.

As she reached the edge of the valley and started to climb again, the ground beneath her turned from sandy dirt to sandstone, and she slowed her horse to allow it to gain purchase on the rocky terrain. There were several granite formations and a mixture of firs and pines, and the higher she went, the slower her progress. Her breath was coming in gasps, and her grip tightened against the reins. Surely the truck and horse trailer was just over this rise and she was almost at her destination.

The horse stumbled, its hooves sliding among the rocks. Luann had never had much opportunity to ride horses. She'd gone to horse camp one summer, but that was about it. As her mount continued to climb the rocky slope, it slipped and stumbled, and finally, there was no way Luann could stay in the saddle. She ended up on the ground, hitting hard and sliding several feet down the slope herself as the gelding faltered away from her. She reached out to grab for the reins, but the horse moved quickly and was soon trotting away from her and back down the incline to the valley below at a rather speedy clip.

Panic swamped Luann, and she scrambled as fast as she could behind an outcrop of rocks. Surely the shooter had seen her fall, and if he hadn't, he had to have seen her riderless horse hurrying across the desert landscape. As if reading her thoughts, a bullet whizzed by her ear and hit the rock behind her, only inches away. She ducked and heard the ricochet, landing hard on her stomach in her attempt to use the boulders as a shield. Without a horse, she didn't know how she stood any chance at all against the madman with the gun.

She scooted back as far as she could, her body pressed against the rock. Had Joaquin seen her fall? Would he come to her rescue or was he too far away to help? Dread swelled within her as her life seemed to pass before her eyes. Cold from the ground seeped into her muscles, making her position even more uncomfortable, even though the granite boulders partially blocked the wind.

Luann started to pray, asking God to save her and Joaquin. She didn't know how, but she knew He was able.

She heard a noise and recognized it as a horse's hoof on the rocks. Had her horse returned, or was Joaquin closer than she'd thought? Indecision held her frozen in place. She was afraid to rise up in case the rider nearby was a foe rather than a friend.

"I know you're back there," said a deep male voice that sounded nothing like Joaquin's. "Come on out with your hands up, and I won't hurt you," he demanded roughly.

She didn't believe a word of it. Her breath came in gasps. Did she have only minutes to live? Despite the cold, she felt tiny beads of perspiration forming on her brow.

"I said come out now!" he said again, this time his voice tinged with impatience. "Your friend is gone. It's just you and me now," he continued. "The harder you make it on me, the worse it will be for you."

Indecision continued to plague her. Should she make him dismount and come behind the rocks to find her? His horse couldn't make it to where she was hiding, but once he dismounted, he could easily maneuver to shoot her from a variety of angles. Still, fear and indecisiveness held her frozen in place. She didn't want to make it easy on him. If he was going to kill her today, she wanted to make it as hard as possible for him to achieve his objective.

He was getting closer. She heard the horse nicker, and the creak of leather as he shifted in the saddle. "You're going to die today," the man continued, his tone matter of fact. "But if you don't show yourself right now, I'll hunt down your mother and kill her, too," the voice threatened.

He knew her mother? That got her. Her mother would suffer enough upon hearing of her only child's death. She couldn't take the chance that the shooter was only spouting empty threats. She had to do whatever she could to keep her mother safe.

"You don't know anything about her," Luann yelled.

"I know her name is Theresa St. John, and where she lives. I also know she's battling cancer," the man responded. "I'm not playing games. I mean what I say."

"How do I know you won't go after her anyway, no matter what I do?" she asked loudly. If she kept the man talking, would Joaquin arrive on the scene? She had no idea where Joaquin was, or if he was even aware of her situation, but she still tried to stall as long as possible.

"You don't, but I give you my word."

"And I'm supposed to trust the word of a murderer?"

The male voice laughed, a low, jagged sound that scraped against the silence. There was nothing amusing about it—it was obviously the laugh of a man who believed he had already won. "You do have a point," he drawled, "but you don't really have any choice now, do you?"

He paused, and Luann heard the restless shift of his horse on the loose rocks, hooves grinding against stone. The sound made her skin prickle. Then his voice came again, colder this time, almost casual. "She's going to die soon anyway. If you do what I want, I won't need to hunt her down. I promise I'll stay away."

Luann's stomach dropped. Her mother. His words slashed through her like a blade, cruel and calculated. If there was even the smallest chance—one sliver of hope—that she could save her mom from a brutal death, she had no choice but to try. Her throat tightened, but she forced herself to move. Slowly, deliberately, she pushed up onto her hands and knees, then rose to her feet, palms lifted in surrender.

She turned toward the gunman. He sat high in the saddle on a hulking brown gelding, the brim of a tan cowboy hat casting his face in shadow. A dark leather jacket clung to his broad frame, the barrel of his rifle unwavering as it tracked her every movement.

Luann studied him with desperate intensity, searching for anything familiar, anything that might explain why he was after her. His scruffy beard masked half his face, but not the hard slash of his mouth or the gleam in his narrow black eyes. Beneath the hat's shadow, his dark brow furrowed—and then his lips curled into a slow, sinister grin.

"I'm so glad you decided to be reasonable," he said, his voice a low rumble that vibrated in her chest. The rifle lifted, steady, aimed directly at her heart.

His grin widened, merciless. "Goodbye, Luann St. John."

THIRTEEN

"Drop the gun," Joaquin ordered as he walked into view, his own Colt poised and ready to shoot. He was pretty far down the mountain and away from the scene unfolding in front of him, but he infused his voice with a firm tone of authority, and he was an excellent shot. The criminal was definitely in his range. Joaquin had dismounted because he'd chosen stealth over distance, and his plan had worked. He'd managed to sneak up on the gunman but hadn't been able to get close enough to get between them before the man had aimed his rifle at Luann. His heart clenched at the sight.

The cowboy turned his head but didn't lower his rifle. "Not a chance," he answered smoothly. "I've tried over and over to finish this job." He motioned with his gun. "This ends today." He glanced at Joaquin again. "I'm usually a decent shot. I might even have time to get you both before you can get off the first bullet."

"It will be the last shot you ever take," Joaquin replied. "I'm a pretty good shot myself."

"You could miss," the mounted man replied. "The accurate range of your pistol is only around a hundred feet."

Joaquin shook his head. "Are you willing to bet your

life on that? This is a really nice 9 mm, and it can reach one hundred and fifty feet without a problem. Not to mention the fact that I spend a fair amount of time on the range." He kept moving closer, but knew the cowboy spoke the truth. He was still a good two hundred feet away, and he doubted he could make an accurate shot that would stop the man before he hurt Luann. Panic and fear warred for supremacy. He didn't know much, but he knew he couldn't lose Luann. It would devastate him.

"Say goodbye to your friend, Sheriff," the cowboy said as he turned toward Luann again. His finger flexed on the trigger, and Joaquin aimed, ready to fire himself.

Suddenly, a growl sounded and Lobo appeared on the scene, running at the gunman. The dog bounded up a nearby rock and soared through the air, his teeth bared.

The cowboy dropped his rifle and put up his arms, reflexively protecting his face from the dog's teeth. The force of the husky hitting him knocked him off his horse, and both dog and cowboy hit the rocky ground with a thud. The two rolled, Lobo attacking with a frenzy of fangs and snarls, but somehow the man got the upper hand and, with a yelp, Lobo was thrown off and sliding along the rocks. It took the husky a moment to regroup, and the cowboy quickly grabbed the rifle and stood, aiming once again for Luann, who seemed frozen by the tableau unfolding in front of her.

"Goodbye, Luann," he said loudly.

A shot sounded and echoed down the valley. Luann's eyes rounded and she froze.

The cowboy looked down at his chest, shock suffusing his features as he noticed the red circle forming on his chest. The rifle fell from his hands and then he slowly pitched forward, dead before he even hit the ground.

Joaquin holstered his weapon and quickly closed the remaining distance between himself and the gunman at a run. He reached down and pulled the rifle away from the cowboy's body, then touched the man's neck, searching for a pulse. There was none. He adjusted his fingers but still felt nothing.

The man was dead.

Joaquin stood and turned to Luann. Her face was wet with tears. Was she still scared, or was she crying for the dead man who had tried to kill her? The reasons didn't matter. He hurried to her side and took her into his arms. A moment later, Lobo joined them and Joaquin reached down and petted his head affectionately.

"I'm so thankful you're safe," he said roughly, unable to keep the emotion out of his voice.

"Yes, and thank you for saving my life," she whispered back. "I thought I was dead for sure." She reached for Lobo and patted him as well. "You and Lobo both. Is Lobo okay?"

"He's fine," Joaquin confirmed. "He's a real tough guy. I told you he thought he was a real police dog."

Luann was quiet for a moment, then added, "I've never been so scared before. I thought he would kill me for sure."

Joaquin couldn't help himself. They'd both just survived a horrendous experience. He desperately needed an affirmation of life. With slow deliberation, he pushed his cowboy hat back, then bent and moved toward her lips, giving her plenty of time to refuse him. Instead of turning away, she met his kiss and kissed him back. It was tender and sweet. Joaquin felt like his insides were shaking right down to his toes. He drew his finger down her cheek, amazed at the softness of her skin.

"I'm sorry," Joaquin said quickly. "I shouldn't have done that."

"Don't apologize," she said as she looked up into his eyes. "I wanted you to kiss me, and I wanted to kiss you." She acted as if she was going to say something more but didn't. It was as if he could see the thoughts swirling in her head. Finally, she pulled back and motioned to the body, as if deciding that it was time to focus back on the case instead of on the kiss they'd just shared. Once again, he noticed a strength within her that he hadn't seen when they'd first met. He liked to see that steel in her eyes in times of adversity. It was incredibly attractive.

"I still don't know his motive. Why would he want to kill me? He knew my name and everything. He even knew my mom has cancer. Why would he know that?"

"It sounds like someone paid him to do the job. My guess is he learned as much as he could about you so he'd know the best way to complete his contract. And it worked—when he threatened your mom, he got what he wanted." He pulled the brim of his hat back down. "You're asking the right questions. We need to find out why he was hired in the first place."

Luann walked over to him and studied the man's face. "That's the same guy I saw in the parking lot at the bed-and-breakfast. I'm pretty sure anyway. It was kind of dark."

"I think it's probably the same guy from the library, too. When we check, I imagine we'll find that he owns or has access to a silver Ford F-150. Actually, I'm hoping he's been the lone shooter all along."

"Do you recognize him?" Luann asked.

"No, I've never seen him before. I imagine he's a gun for hire—he might even be from Albuquerque." Joaquin pulled out his phone and checked the screen. "No service. I was afraid of that." He took a photo of the dead man's face, and several other photos of the crime scene and surrounding area from different angles. It was rough terrain, which would make it difficult to retrieve the body, but it would have to be done.

He then used his phone's GPS, which operated separately from the cell networks, to mark the man's location with specific coordinates. He would have to send up a team and a pathologist. He wished he had a blanket or tarp or something he could use to cover up the man's body, but he had nothing. He found a piece of wood that was over six feet long and dug it into the ground, resembling a flagpole of sorts, hoping it would help him find the body when he returned. The man's horse had run off, and Joaquin's own horse had also pulled free and run away, presumably due to the gunfire. Even Luann's gelding had disappeared. It looked like they'd be walking back to the truck.

"Let's get back to the pickup," Joaquin said, giving the scene one last look. He considered his options—he hoped animals wouldn't mess with the body right away, but he really didn't see that he had any choice but to leave the man lying where he'd fallen until he could return with help. Taking care of the living took precedence over taking care of the dead—especially when the deceased was a would-be killer.

"It will take us a while. I lost my horse," Luann said quietly.

"That's okay. I lost mine, too. I imagine we'll find them both either back at the truck or at their stables. Either way, until I can get service, we'll be on foot."

Luann had also pulled out her phone and was looking at her screen. She frowned. "There has to be service out here somewhere. We'll just have to keep trying as we go."

"Agreed," Joaquin said with a nod. He motioned to the west and studied the sun. "If we start now, we should make it to the truck before dark. Once I get you settled, I'll have to return with a team and lights to retrieve the body."

"I sure hope we get there before the sun goes down," Luann intoned as she rubbed her arms. "I guess the adrenaline is starting to dissipate, because suddenly I'm cold. When we come back up to search those three grid sections, we'll have to bring some even better cold-weather supplies. I thought this coat and gloves would do it, but I'm still a bit chilly."

"We'll make it," Joaquin reassured her. "You know the desert—warm during the day and really cold during the night, especially now during the fall."

They were quiet for a few minutes as they walked, then Luann spoke up. "You know, I don't know how I could have survived everything that's happened without God. I was praying constantly. I have to give Him credit for saving us, not just now, but even yesterday and the day before." She paused. "Do you believe in God?"

Joaquin nodded. "Yes, I'm a Christian. There's a little chapel in town where Camila and I go, when I can. Sometimes the job interferes, though, and I have to work on

Sundays." His thoughts turned to his church community. "You know, that's one of the really nice things about living in a small town like this. We're a close-knit group, and we share a lot of the same values and beliefs. We're a rural area, and we all know each other and hang out together in good times and bad. Our faith pulls us closer together."

"I agree," Luann said quietly. "Except when an outsider comes like me, asking questions. Then the friendliness seems to dry up a little. But Gary was incredibly nice, and Susanna and Ted have been amazing." She met his eyes. "And, of course, you've been the best of them all. I can't believe how much you've helped me."

He smiled and thought about her words for a moment. He appreciated her praise, but she did make a good point. "You're right about our little town," he finally admitted. "Del Norte does need to open up a bit more to outsiders. I guess we're a little suspicious of strangers. A while back, three years or so I'd guess, there were these two couples that came to town. We welcomed them in, showed them around, and then it turned out they'd lied to us all and were actually real-estate developers. They didn't tell us their plans at first, but after a few days, it was clear that they were going to destroy our little town and make it into some sort of hidden destination resort. In fact, they downright lied about their motives and tried to turn neighbor against neighbor to get what they wanted. I really never understood all of their plans, but the hype was pretty over-the-top. The local folks had to basically band together and refuse to sell. Ever since then, we've been a suspicious lot."

Luann considered Joaquin's comments and instantly reconsidered her opinion. She had been quick to judge without really knowing the other side, and that had been wrong of her. She thought back over the conversations she'd had when she'd first arrived through the lens of the new information that Joaquin had provided. "That's horrible. No wonder they're so suspicious."

They walked in silence again for a while, and then she spoke up. "I'm really glad you told me that. I just assumed most everyone was unfriendly, but that was a bad assumption on my part. I should have asked." She tilted her head. "I'm sorry I jumped to conclusions without finding out the truth. It probably didn't help that, when people asked why I was visiting, I didn't go into much detail. They probably thought I was hiding something, when really I just didn't know where to start to find out about the crash." She smiled. "It's a good lesson for me. Never assume."

"We can all learn something," Joaquin agreed. "Jesus made it pretty clear we're supposed to love our neighbor. There's no ambiguity in that command."

They continued walking with Lobo close at their heels. About every fifteen minutes, they stopped and checked their cell service to see if there was any improvement. After the third time, Joaquin was able to get one bar, and he quickly called in his team and the coordinates of the body.

They made it back to the truck and trailer just a short time later. Both of Levi's horses were waiting near the truck, munching on some grass. Luann and Joaquin loaded the horses and took them back to Levi's ranch.

Levi met them with a knowing look on his face. "It was a rough ride, right? Just like I told you."

"It was rough because someone was trying to kill me,

not because of the terrain," Luann clarified, still somewhat annoyed at the man's attitude.

Levi looked genuinely surprised by her words, and even more flummoxed when the sheriff pulled out his phone and showed the older man the photo of the shooter's face. "Do you recognize this man?"

Levi looked but shook his head. "No. I don't think he's from around these parts." He scratched his head. "Is he dead?"

"He is," Joaquin confirmed. "Are you sure he doesn't look familiar?"

"I'm sure," Levi nodded. "I've never seen the man. You can ask the ranch hands if you want. Maybe one of them has seen him around." He chewed the inside of his cheek. "What happened out there?"

"That man followed us and tried to kill us," Joaquin stated flatly. "He was shooting at us with a rifle, but it didn't turn out the way he planned." He pointed toward the barn. "I've got a team coming up to retrieve the body. We're going to need some more horses."

"Whatever you need," Levi agreed. "I'm happy to help."

Joaquin nodded his appreciation and pocketed his phone just as his team drove up. He quickly explained his plan and organized his team.

Luann watched from where she stood by the corral and tried to stay out of his way. She found herself enjoying seeing him work. He was obviously respected by his colleagues, and as she'd thought from the beginning, he was easy on the eyes, especially wearing that brown Stetson. Finally, when he was ready to go, he came over to the corral to say goodbye, with Ricky at his side. "I have to go back up there to retrieve the body of the shooter, but I've asked Ricky to stay with you until I can get back, okay? He'll drive you to the bed-and-breakfast and keep an eye on things."

She glanced over at the deputy. She wished that Joaquin could come, but she understood that he needed to work. He was the sheriff, after all. She gave Ricky a tentative smile. "I'd love for Ricky to help me out, but can you spare him? I mean, you're going to need all hands on deck, and the shooter is dead. That probably means the threat is over. I can drive the Camry back over to Susanna's without a problem."

Joaquin shook his head. "We don't know that, Luann. Until we know the motive behind the attempts on your life, I want to make sure you're safe." Their eyes met and she could see his determination and caring. This was one battle she wasn't going to win.

She capitulated. "Okay, I understand. Thanks for being so careful and considerate with my welfare."

Joaquin tipped his hat, then turned. She watched him return to a group of men and women, standing with Levi, who were undoubtedly planning their trip to the crime scene. Yep. He was easy on the eyes alright. But what made Joaquin attractive was more than just his outward appearance. He had a heart of gold. It was easy to see in everything he did, from the way he took charge of his men to the way he hugged his little girl. His ex-wife had been foolish to desert him.

She glanced at the field by the barn and was surprised to see a lone brown gelding there, walking along the fence line inside the paddock and eating grass. The horse had a white blaze across his face and looked a lot like the horse the shooter had been riding. Brown horses were common, but this one even looked like it was the same size as the one she'd seen earlier and it had the same white sock on his left foreleg.

Had Levi also rented a horse to the shooter? Or was that man's horse still out there, wandering around the desert?

A cold chill swept up her spine. Even if he had rented the animal, that didn't mean Levi was involved in any way in trying to harm her. She looked for Levi around the barnyard and saw him talking to another large, white-haired man who appeared to work for him as a ranch hand. Both men wore similar clothing, including jeans, boots and sheepskin jackets. The two seemed deep in conversation, but she had no idea what they were talking about.

She went back over her previous conversations with the ranch owner. Levi had claimed he'd never seen the shooter before. But did Levi participate in every rental that occurred on his property? Wasn't it possible that, if the killer had gotten his horse from Levi's ranch, he'd rented the horse through one of Levi's employees? She didn't want to be paranoid and suspicious, but she also didn't want to do something stupid because she wasn't paying attention to the little details around her.

Despite the fact that the shooter was dead, Luann couldn't get over the sensation that she was still being watched. Even the fine hairs on her arm were standing on end as she looked around the barnyard and corral. She didn't see anyone suspicious, but she freely admitted she was no trained investigator. She wasn't sure she could spot danger or react as quickly as Joaquin when a threat appeared.

Thoughts continued to whirl in her head. Would whoever had hired the man to kill her hire someone else, now that the original shooter had been killed? Would she ever be able to relax again?

One thing Luann did know—she couldn't leave the ranch soon enough. When Ricky pulled up in the Camry, she quickly jumped inside and locked the door as if that would somehow keep her horrible thoughts and what-ifs on the outside of the vehicle. It took a good hour or so to get to Del Norte, and they drove in virtual silence. Once they arrived, Luann felt exhaustion come over her like she could sleep for a week.

"So, you're okay?" Ricky asked once they reached the hallway by her room.

"Yes, thanks, Ricky, for bringing me back and staying nearby. I really appreciate it." She opened her room door, then stepped back, stunned.

Ricky noticed her distress and pulled his sidearm, then stepped protectively in front of her. His eyes darted around the area and slowly he made his way into the small room, gun at the ready. A moment later, he came back to the doorway. "Clear," he reported as he holstered his weapon. "Whoever did this is gone."

Luann still couldn't catch her breath as she looked over Ricky's shoulder.

The entire room had been ransacked. Furniture had been strewn about, and everything of value seemed to have been destroyed. The curtains were pulled from the rods, and a pillow had been sliced open, feathers covering everything.

This case was far from over.

FOURTEEN

Luann sipped her hot tea, leaned back in her chair in the bed-and-breakfast dining room and sighed. She'd had a rough night, seeing the shooter's threatening stance as he pointed a rifle at her chest over and over again in her mind's eye. Thankfully, she had eventually gotten a few hours of sleep, but she was still struggling as the stress of the last few days pulled against her. Now that she was up, she continued to think through all of the different facets of the case. Somebody clearly didn't want her to continue the search for the truth, but instead of scaring her off, the threats made her even more determined. After all, they wouldn't be trying to kill her if she wasn't trying to uncover a secret that somebody obviously wanted to remain hidden. Instinctively, even though she had no proof, she knew that whatever secret that was, it had to do with her father and the plane that had crashed into the mountainside so many years ago. She had checked in with her mom via phone, and the call had bolstered her resolve even further. Her mother's condition was deteriorating. She had to find the truth before her mother died, and time was running out.

"There you are," Joaquin said with a smile as he poured

a cup of coffee at the hot-drink bar and brought it over to her table.

"Welcome back," Luann said. She couldn't help it. Just seeing him there, a day's growth of beard on his face, made her remember not only how he had saved her life, but also the kiss they had shared on the mountainside afterward. She tried to push the thoughts aside, but images kept returning, unbidden—the sweetness of the kiss, the softness of his lips…

"Thanks. I heard you had some excitement while I was gone."

"Yeah," Luann nodded, taking another sip of her tea. "Someone decided to redecorate my room."

"Anything damaged that can't be replaced?"

"My laptop was stolen, but I always back up everything on the cloud, so it will be expensive to replace, but I didn't really lose anything."

"I'm so sorry that happened."

"Me, too. Susanna lost a couple of antique lamps and some nice bed linens and curtains, but they can all be replaced. It was more of mess than anything." She took another sip of tea. "Any news about the shooter?"

Joaquin shook his head. "No. I've got two deputies searching for his identity and background, but so far, we haven't even gotten a name for him, which means we also have no idea who hired him. His fingerprints aren't on record anywhere, and his face didn't pop on any facial recognition databases we have access to. We're still looking for his vehicle."

"Well, I've been thinking a lot about the entire case, and I have a theory." She put her cup down on the table.

Joaquin smiled at her and leaned forward. "I'm all ears."

"Well, I think someone else knows the story of the diamond theft, and also thinks those diamonds were on that plane. I think Fabio was looking for the diamonds, and he had a partner—a greedy partner who killed him because he was afraid Fabio would talk to me."

Joaquin rubbed his chin. "You could be right." He pulled out his phone and blew up the picture of the map from Fabio's house. "If he did have a partner, Fabio and that unknown person have probably been searching for the diamonds for the past several years and have searched all of the areas marked except the three remaining grid squares. That fits your theory. It would have taken a long time to do a thorough search of the area. We're talking several square miles, and if he was looking for diamonds, it's no wonder it's taken so many years—it's almost an impossible task. It is conceivable that even if all of this is true, the diamonds might still never be found." He leaned back. "Your theory makes sense, based on everything that has happened. I'm guessing the partner hired the killer to either scare you off or get rid of you completely."

"I agree. He didn't like that I was asking questions. If the diamonds are out there, he wants them all to himself. The question is, how did the partner even know of the diamonds' existence, and the connection between the diamonds and the crash? I mean, the pilot died. No one survived that crash. Who else knew the diamonds could have been on that plane? We're still missing pieces of the story."

"Those are great questions, and ones I can't answer. If they were worth two million twenty years ago, you know they're worth a whole lot more now."

Luann shrugged. "You know, the irony is I don't even care about the stones. All I want is to know what happened to my father. I'd leave here tomorrow if I could just discover the truth."

"Would you?" Joaquin asked softly. "Would you leave here tomorrow?" There was a wistful tone to his voice, and he quickly turned away, then stood and walked out on the porch before Luann could read his expression.

She wondered what he meant by that, but it was obvious that he didn't want to continue the conversation. Had he been hurt by her comment? Surely he knew that she wouldn't be staying in Del Norte once her investigation was over. Yet she felt a pang of regret every time she thought about going back home all alone. She and Joaquin had forged a bond over the last few days, one that was growing stronger with each passing hour. Yet hadn't she been determined *not* to start a relationship with anyone? In her book, long-distance romance never worked. It was even more impossible than trying to have a relationship survive with someone who lived in the local area. Still, despite her misgivings, she couldn't seem to get Joaquin out of her mind.

She drained her cup, then went to apologize for her thoughtless comment. She didn't have to figure everything out today, but she did need to make sure that Joaquin knew how much she appreciated all he had done and was continuing to do for her. She found Joaquin on the front porch, talking on the phone. Before she could say a word, he hung up and turned to her, his face animated.

"Good news. Levi has everything we need for another trail ride up to check out those three remaining grids.

He's waiting for us and will trailer the horses as soon as we get there."

Luann raised an eyebrow. "Do you trust Levi?"

Joaquin paused for a moment and turned his cowboy hat around and around in his hand. "I never thought about it before. He's been a Del Norte resident for years, and I've never had a problem with him. Why do you ask?"

"Because yesterday, I saw a large brown horse in the field by his barn, and it looked an awful lot like the horse the shooter was riding. He even had a blaze on his face and a sock on his left front foot. It made me wonder if Levi knew the shooter and rented him a horse." She lowered her voice. "Or if he was even the one who hired the shooter..."

Joaquin put his hands on his hips. "Are you sure about the horse?"

"Positive. It has very distinctive markings."

Joaquin paced back and forth for a moment, then turned back to her, his face grim. "I'll have a deputy start running a check on his background, just to see if any red flags pop up." He pulled out his phone. "And let's take another look when we get there before we hit the trail. Maybe we'll see some clues that can help us decide one way or another whether or not Levi is a threat." He shook his head. "I'd hate for him to be involved. He's a leader in this town, and has always been involved in all sorts of civic projects."

"Maybe he has the most to lose if we discover he's responsible for Fabio's death."

Joaquin let Luann's words ruminate through his mind as they grabbed their coats, loaded the car and headed back up to Levi's ranch. He hated the idea of Levi being a criminal, but he would do his job if the evidence pointed in Levi's direction.

Could Levi be a killer? Could he have killed Fabio, and hired someone to shoot Luann? Did that mean Carlos was involved, too?

Once they arrived at the ranch, Levi was once again waiting for them out by the corral. His large, older ranch hand, Mr. Carballo, started loading the horses into the trailer as soon as Joaquin and Luann parked.

"I packed equipment for two nights, even though you said you would probably only be out for one," Levi said as they left Mr. Carballo working with the horses. "You've got tents, bedrolls, food and water, and of course, I'll need you to feed and water the horses while you're gone." He pulled out a paper map and marked where a stream ran through the area, then pointed at various locations. "If you stay along here, you'll probably have good spots to set up camp that are close to the water."

Joaquin made a mental note of Levi's demeanor. He didn't seem bothered by their quest, or nearly as interested as he had been in their last trip, when he had clearly tried to discourage them. He glanced around the ranch but didn't catch sight of any horses in the corral where Luann had previously seen the large brown gelding she'd described. He motioned toward the corral. "You had a horse back there the last time we were here, but I don't see him now."

"I move animals around all the time," Levi said casually. "Was there a reason you're asking?"

"The horse looked familiar, that's all."

Levi shrugged. "What did the horse look like?"

"It was large brown gelding with a white blaze and a white sock."

Levi tilted his head as if he were trying to remember. "Didn't belong to me, I don't think, anyway. I'm pretty sure I don't have a horse like that. I'm not sure why he was in my corral. But like I said, we move animals around a lot. I can ask the workers about it if you are really interested."

It was Joaquin's turn to shrug. He didn't want to make Levi suspicious, and if Levi wasn't involved, he didn't want to alert the killer that they were aware of the horse's whereabouts. He felt it was better to investigate the horse issue more once they had finished their trail trip. He trusted Luann's sighting of the horse, but Levi did operate a big operation, and like he'd admitted, horses got moved around on a regular basis. He would let it go for now, but it was definitely a line of inquiry that Joaquin wanted to follow up on when he returned. "It's probably not a big deal. I was just curious, that's all. It was a nice-looking gelding."

"You in the market for a horse of your own?" Levi asked. "You know that daughter of yours is going to be asking for her own horse soon, if she hasn't started asking already."

Joaquin laughed. "Thankfully, she's still into princesses, but I think the horse phase is coming. I'll let you know if I'm ever in the market."

"Sounds like a plan," Levi agreed.

Joaquin watched the man walk toward the ranch house. He hadn't seen Carlos Sanchez lately and was wondering if Levi knew whether or not his son had access to a silver pickup. This was another line of inquiry he wanted to follow after the grid search. One thing at a time, though. He felt driven to explore those three remaining grids, as if they were calling him, begging him to discover their secrets. The thought was pure foolishness, but he still felt confident they were going to discover something during this trip—anything would be welcome that helped them understand more about what had actually happened to Luann's dad.

They got in the truck and pulled out, the horses ensconced in the trailer. Joaquin was glad that Levi had rented trail ride supplies along with the horses, because it had been a while since he'd gone camping, and he hadn't had to worry about finding his gear or figuring out a packing list.

He tipped his hat at Mr. Carballo, who was smiling at them and gave them a friendly wave as they drove through the gate. He didn't know Mr. Carballo well, but he'd always been friendly, albeit rather quiet. The older man didn't seem to like notoriety and was usually working in the background somewhere instead of drawing attention to himself. He was a tall, muscular man in his early sixties and usually sported an attractive pair of ornate highly polished cowboy boots when he wasn't working. He undoubtedly did a lot of manual labor around the ranch and seemed to be an expert that the other hands turned to when they had questions.

Joaquin put thoughts of Mr. Carballo behind him and focused on his driving. In about an hour, they made it to the rural location where Levi had marked the map, and were soon on their horses and riding toward the three grids that Fabio had not had a chance to mark on his map. Lobo followed closely behind. The dog had no trouble keeping up and spent a great deal of time sniffing the plants and ground as if a rabbit were nearby.

Joaquin hoped they would find something, anything, that would shine more light on the case, but even if their efforts proved fruitless, he couldn't regret taking another chance to spend time with Luann, or to bring her any small measure of closure in her father's case.

Two hours later, they were still riding and had said very little. Both seemed lost in their own thoughts but were also enjoying the landscape and the beautiful New Mexico mountain. Joaquin was comfortable with the silence between them and didn't feel the need to chatter just to fill the space. He glanced over at her as she rode a handsome sorrel gelding with a small white star on his forehead. He had to admit that he'd been thrown by her offhanded comment that she would be leaving soon. He knew it. She'd only planned to be in Del Norte for a few days. Still, he just hadn't accepted it. For some reason, he was starting to feel like Luann belonged in Del Norte with him at her side.

It was a foolish thought. After all, he'd only known her for a few days.

She was so beautiful on the outside—he'd known that from the beginning. Her eyes were flecked with a lovely gray and so expressive he felt like he could almost read her thoughts by just glancing in her direction. Her dark brown hair was wavy, with just a touch of red highlights that made it shimmer in the sun, and her wide lips and high cheekbones gave her both a classy and friendly appearance. He was entranced. But it was more than her looks that he found appealing. Now he was seeing a beauty on her inside that made him rethink his decision to never date again and to raise Camila alone.

He tried not to compare Luann to the woman who had abandoned him, but it was nearly impossible not to. His ex-wife had been beautiful on the outside, too, but also incredibly self-absorbed and always wanting more of anything she felt was owed to her.

Luann thought of others first and put their needs and wants above her own. It was evident in her words and her actions. She was the complete package.

Was God giving him a second chance with Luann? He'd thought it was impossible, yet here he was, thinking of that kiss he had given her, and the softness of her skin when he had dared to touch her hand. In his mind's eye, he could see himself waiting at the altar, seeing Camila as a flower girl, followed in by Luann in a lovely white gown…

"I'm not that great at reading maps," Luann said lightly as her voice broke into his thoughts. "Do you think we're close?"

Joaquin pointed toward a ravine in the distance. "I think I understand now why Fabio saved these sectors for last. See that area over there? That's where we're headed. Not only are these regions hard to get to, but they are filled with ravines and trees that are virtually untouched. We'll be moving even slower once we get closer." He glanced at the sky, enjoying the heat from the sun as he stretched a bit in the saddle. "The crash site we visited yesterday is pretty far from these two sections. It's doubtful we'll find anything."

"I'm aware," Luann replied with a smile. "But I have to check every box. We're assuming that Fabio did a thorough job of searching the other areas and never found anything, but I think it's a safe assumption that he never found anything since we never heard of any discoveries in the area." She tilted her head. "Don't you think the media would have picked up on something if Fabio and his partner had found the diamonds, or even something smaller like more parts of the plane?"

"Yes, it's hard to keep a secret of any kind in this day and age. And Del Norte is so small that even a tiny discovery would have made it through the town's grapevine. But you also have to remember, Fabio is just one man, and he was searching a large area. He very well could have missed any clues, even if he did his very best during the search."

A horse neighed in the distance, and Joaquin was instantly on alert. They were in a very remote area and there shouldn't be anybody else around.

Were they being followed again? Was there a second killer nearby, just waiting for a chance to end both their quest and their lives?

FIFTEEN

The next morning, the two rose early and brewed some hot tea over a small campfire. Luann handed Joaquin a granola bar from their food pack, and a shiny green Granny Smith. He took them both with a smile and sat down on a nearby rock. He had mentioned that he'd thought he'd heard a horse in the distance the evening before, but neither one of them had heard anything else since. Still, they stayed alert and focused on the objective at hand. Luann could tell Joaquin was still being watchful of their surroundings, and they had slept in shifts during the night, one of them keeping watch against wild animals and humans, just in case someone or something approached them. And of course, Lobo was always on duty.

Joaquin took a bite of his apple. "Not exactly the same caliber as the food at the bed-and-breakfast, is it?"

Luann laughed. "I'm probably a really lousy camp cook. You're better off with what I just gave you than anything I could prepare over a fire."

"Not even s'mores?" Joaquin teased.

"Well, now that you've tossed chocolate into the mix, that brings all sorts of new possibilities."

He laughed as she opened her own granola bar and took a bite.

The evening had been uneventful, but that was the way Luann liked it. The little tents and sleeping bags Levi had provided had come in very small packages, but were amazingly warm, and she had slept better than she'd thought she would.

Joaquin ate quickly and was soon untying the horses from the highline, or "picket line" as some people called it, that was stretched between two trees. By tying the horses' halters to the line, the animals were able to move about in a safe and contained area, but they were also prevented from wandering off, damaging trees or getting tangled. Joaquin had also explained that the highline minimized the environmental impact of camping outdoors with the large animals. Luann was all for being environmentally conscious and doing all she could to protect this rugged and beautiful country. She loved New Mexico, with the skies that seemed to go on forever and the rugged beauty of the mountains and desert. Her mind returned fleetingly to the gunman who had tried to take her life yesterday, but she did her best to push those memories aside. She was alive right here, right now, and she would do her best to enjoy every minute she could.

Luann and Joaquin spent the better part of the morning and early afternoon searching the first two grids and found nothing of interest. The search was slow going, and the land was difficult to traverse. A deep ravine cut one of the grids in two, but thankfully, the horse she had this time was better suited for the rocky terrain and much more sure-footed, so he didn't slip as much as the horse she'd ridden yesterday.

After several hours had passed and they'd stopped for lunch, Luann was starting to wonder if she was on a fool's errand. What could she possibly find in these mountain woods twenty years after a crash that had left very little behind? It was a small plane, after all, and the NTSB report had found and documented most of the pieces of the plane at the crash site. What was she really hoping to discover? Yet she was driven in her search and urged herself onward.

By midafternoon, Luann was even more tired and frustrated. She wasn't used to being in the saddle for hours at a time, and the muscles in her legs and core were protesting. She stopped her horse and pulled out her canteen for a quick drink. Joaquin was about fifty feet behind her, still searching among the trees. She had to admit, he had been a wonderful traveling companion. He was letting her take the lead, and hadn't once complained about the ride, the rocky conditions or the fact that her search was taking him away from his normal sheriff duties and his daughter. She knew she was being a burden, and that he wouldn't be able to continue the search much longer after they finished checking these three map grids. He had to get back to his normal duties, and honestly, she had to return to her work as well. She wasn't wealthy, and this trip had cut into her savings. She had also already been assigned her next set of classes to teach at the community college back in Clovis, and the express courses started next week.

She glanced at the tall ponderosa pines and the beautiful landscape of the Sandia Mountains and shifted in her saddle. She had to face the facts. After these three grids, she was done. She had no other leads—nothing else to follow up on or to investigate. She knew a moment of angst as she considered her father and once again remembered images of him from her childhood.

In her mind's eye, she saw him reaching down and hugging her after she had fallen off her bike and scraped her knee. He had been a caring father—one involved in her life who took the time to read books to her at night and to be invested in her young life. She'd missed him so much and felt a pang of regret that he'd never been there to celebrate the milestones—her graduations from high school and college, when she'd won the English award her freshman year, when she'd gotten her first magazine article published or when she'd landed her first teaching job. She ached to share those things with him and more but would never get the chance. Now, it seemed, she would also never know what happened to him, and her mother would die heartbroken and alone, since her heart still belonged to her missing husband and always would.

Luann took a deep breath and studied the area. She had to focus on the here and now. The tree line opened up in front of her and led into a clearing about the size of a baseball field, covered in blue grama and little bluestems. More pines and firs led up the mountainside on the other side of the wide-open area, with a variety of granite boulders and brush sprinkled throughout the tall trunks. The mountainside in this grid was thick with vegetation, and it had been slow going, yet the landscape was filled with beauty that reminded her of God's majesty.

It was time to pray. She closed her eyes for a moment and said a heartfelt prayer of thankfulness. Maybe she wouldn't get the answers she was seeking. But she was finding closure of a different kind. After she finished this trip, she could honestly say to herself and to her mother that she had done everything possible to find out the truth about her father. Had he stolen the diamonds? Had he been on that plane? She didn't know. But the experience of searching for the answers had helped her grow, and she was now ready to face whatever challenges occurred in her future without constantly looking backward.

A horse nickered and she looked up to see Joaquin approaching on his bay. He was smiling and pointing at the sky. "See that? That's not something you come across every day."

Luann followed the direction he was pointing and saw a bald eagle circling in the sky above them. It was a magnificent and regal bird, and she was mesmerized as it soared. She spent about ten minutes just watching it fly around the clearing and was disappointed when it finally flew away and disappeared behind a group of trees.

A motion suddenly caught her eye and she leaned forward in the saddle, trying to get a better view. "What's that?" She pointed north to where the eagle had vanished.

"Where?" Joaquin asked, following her hand. "What do you see?"

"There's something up there at the top of that tree. It looks like a piece of blue fabric." She shielded her eyes with her hand to get a better view, and not being successful, nudged her horse to move to the left.

"I don't see it," he responded, but then he adjusted himself in the saddle. "Oh wait, now I see what you're talking about. I can't tell what I'm looking at, but whatever it is, it isn't supposed to be up there. I can tell you that much." He pulled out a small set of binoculars and focused on the patch of blue that was waving slightly in the breeze.

* * *

Joaquin swallowed as he adjusted the lenses so he could get a better look at the object near the top of the pine tree. A knot formed in his stomach.

It was a skeleton.

The body was still partially clothed, but there wasn't much left of it that he could see besides the bones and what looked like torn bits of a blue jacket and dark pants. After twenty years in New Mexico's arid and exposed environment, the dry hot air had significantly accelerated decomposition, leaving the skin dehydrated and leathery. He saw a bit of dark brown hair but was unable to distinguish any facial or other features. He wasn't sure if the skeleton was completely up in the tree, or if part of it had fallen and been scattered by the elements, the tree's movements or scavenging animals. A few larger bones seemed almost bleached by the sun, but it was impossible to really see them well since they seemed to blend right in with the coloring of the bark and tree branches.

"Oh, Luann," he said with a touch of sadness to his voice that he could do nothing to avoid. Their eyes met and she was suddenly off, riding as quickly as possible toward the tree. It didn't take her long to get there, and she instantly dismounted as soon as she arrived at its base. He followed close behind her and quickly dismounted himself and tied his horse off to a nearby tree branch.

"It's him. I know it. It just has to be him." Her voice cracked as she said the words and she circled the tree trunk, trying to get any sort of view of the body.

"I'm afraid you might be right. There's definitely a body up there," Joaquin agreed.

The skeleton was too high to reach, and it would be

foolhardy to try to climb the tree without some assistance. Joaquin studied the situation critically and started making a list in his head of the equipment a team would need to retrieve the body.

"Look at this!" Luann said with excitement in her voice. She bent down and recovered a wallet and a shoe at the foot of the tree. Both were in horrible shape and had definitely been exposed to the elements for some time. She flipped open the wallet, looked at the contents, and then a sob erupted deep within her.

"It's him. It's my father."

She flew into Joaquin's waiting embrace and he wrapped his arms around her and held her tightly as she cried, letting out all of the pain and sorrow that was no doubt swimming within her. His heart broke to see her pain, yet he was also thankful that they had finally found the answers that she'd been seeking.

"He really is dead," she said as she tried to get control of herself. "You know, a part of me kept picturing him sitting on a beach somewhere in some exotic location, sipping drinks and surfing the waves. I never really believed that he would do something like that, but law enforcement was sure that's what happened. The image of him alive was easier to accept than thinking he was dead and gone."

He held her for a few minutes more, and then she finally pulled away and took a better look at the wallet and its contents. "Here's his driver's license," she said softly. "And here's his health insurance card, his credit card and his gas card." She laughed. "He only had twenty bucks on him. Wow." She held out the wallet and gave it to Joaquin. All of the cards were emblazoned with the name of Henry

St. John. He looked closer at the driver's license photo and could see a man in his mid-thirties with dark brown hair and gray eyes. He was handsome, and he could see where Luann got many of her pleasant features. It was obvious they were related.

He glanced up. The tree where the body was found was at the edge of a narrow ravine and partially protected from the elements due to the shape of the mountain in this particular area. The topography explained a bit about how the bones had survived undiscovered for the last twenty years.

"Do you recognize that?" Joaquin asked as he motioned to the dried-up old shoe in her hand. It had probably been a nice leather penny loafer at one time but was now shriveled and dirty.

"Nope, but I was just a kid when he disappeared. I never really paid attention to what he was wearing. He did usually wear a suit to work, and I'm pretty sure he was wearing a dark suit in those old surveillance videos."

Joaquin nodded then motioned with his hand. "Let's look around the area and see if we find anything else." He suddenly frowned. "You know, I don't see a parachute anywhere—not in the trees or anywhere around here on the ground or stuck in the bushes. That's odd. I'm sure if he'd had one, we'd at least find some evidence of it."

"It was a skydiving plane they were on, but who knows what actually happened up there in the air? That's something we'll probably never know. Maybe he got pushed out or fell out during a scuffle. Maybe there weren't enough parachutes, and he had to just jump and hope he survived before the plane crashed."

She returned to where she had dropped her horse's

reins, tied off her mount, and then started walking around the area, apparently searching for anything else that might have dropped from her father's body. Joaquin battled trepidation as he watched her search. It would undoubtedly be hard for her emotionally to find human bones on the ground, but thankfully, there were just a couple of small bits of bone partially buried in the sandy soil and covered in pine needles. She paused when she reached his side, and he enveloped her in a warm side hug, hoping to lend his support as she dealt with the melee of emotions that he saw fleeting across her face. A few moments later, she gave him a tremulous shrug and continued the search.

They spent a good hour looking around the area but didn't find anything new. Finally, Joaquin put his hands on his hips and called to Luann, who returned to the clearing.

"I don't have service here, and it's getting rather late. We probably only have a few more hours of daylight left anyway. How do you feel about camping here overnight? We can ride back in the morning and send a team back to retrieve your father's body." He paused, trying to be as sensitive as possible. "Do you have a burial plan in mind?"

"I'll have to contact my mother to confirm everything, but yes, let's figure it all out tomorrow. I'm an emotional wreck right now."

"Understandable." Joaquin could see the pain and stress on her face and wanted nothing more than to hold and comfort her. Would she let him? He reached out and slowly drew a finger down her cheek. Her skin was soft, just as he remembered.

She smiled and he let his hand drop. "Thank you for

coming up here with me and protecting me during this search. I really appreciate all that you've done." She pushed some of her hair behind her ear. "Looking back, I'm not sure what I would have done if you hadn't been the sheriff in Del Norte."

He smiled and warmth infused him from head to toe. This lady was indeed something special. How was he going to let her go? "You're welcome. I'll take care of the horses. Can you start a fire? Then I'll see what kind of food we have in that pack for dinner."

She agreed and quickly went to work creating a ring of rocks near a large granite boulder by the edge of the clearing that would block the flames from the wind. Joaquin got the highline set, then took the saddles off the horses, attached their halters to the line, and set them up with food and water from the packs. By the time he was finished, Luann had a nice fire blazing and a pile of firewood nearby that would feed it during the night. Together, they put up the tents and laid out their sleeping bags.

Joaquin had just turned to see what was in the food packs that he could fix for dinner when Lobo came up with something in his mouth. The object was dark brown and weathered.

"What's that, boy? What'd you bring me?" He rubbed the dog's head affectionately, then pulled at the dog's mouth to see what he had.

"Looks like Lobo found your father's other shoe," Joaquin said as Lobo released it into his hands. He turned and showed it to Luann, who compared it to the first one they'd found.

"Yeah, looks like a match. I would imagine that both of them fell off the body at some point due to the wind or something." She turned it over and peered at the opening. "Wait, there's something inside." She pulled out some navy material that looked like an old pair of polyester dress socks. The material was full of holes, and seemed to fall apart as she removed it from the shoe.

"That's weird," Joaquin commented as she gently removed the material. "I wonder why there are two socks in one shoe. It's like he took off his shoes before the crash."

"He did," Luann confirmed as she dug deeper into the weathered leather. Underneath the socks, there was a small plastic bag. The delicate plastic contained a black velvet bag with a drawstring and a folded piece of paper.

Luann's eyes rounded. She slowly opened the velvet bag, which was also brittle with age and exposure. She was careful to keep the contents from falling to the ground, and gently poured from the bag into her palm. A moment later, she found her hand full of small, beautiful diamonds that sparkled in the light from the fire.

"Oh, wow," Joaquin commented, shocked by their discovery. "There really were diamonds on that plane."

SIXTEEN

Luann's tears spilled again, hot and unrelenting. She couldn't stop them; grief and confusion tangled together in her chest, making it impossible to breathe easily. Joaquin noticed immediately. Without a word, he reached into his pocket and pulled out a clean, folded bandana, then pressed it gently into her hands. She wiped at her nose, the fabric rough against her skin, and tried to gather her scattered thoughts.

So…was her father a thief after all?

The question gnawed at her. The missing diamonds, glittering faintly even in the dim light, had been found near what was unmistakably her father's final resting place, carefully tucked into the toe of his shoe. The evidence weighed heavy on her heart, distressing and unrelenting, and doubt slithered in, whispering that the man she'd adored might have been capable of betrayal.

With trembling fingers, she returned the diamonds to the bag, sealing it as best she could, and tucked them back into the shoe. Then she shifted her attention to the letter. The paper was yellowed and brittle with age, edges frayed and wrinkled, but the words remained clear, protected for two decades by the plastic bag that had kept them safe. Her pulse quickened as recognition sparked—her father's handwriting, familiar and intimate, sprawled across the page.

She swallowed hard, bracing herself, and began to read out loud, each word pulling her closer to the truth she had chased for so long.

My dear Theresa and Luann,

If you're reading this letter, I'm almost certainly dead, and you've probably been wondering what happened to me. I went to work today and a man came in and robbed the store. I don't know his name and have never seen him before. He kidnapped me and forced me to go with him to the airport. He said he would come back and kill you both if I didn't cooperate, so I didn't have any choice. I couldn't let him hurt you. I had to do whatever I could to make sure you were both safe. He jumped with the only parachute, and I'm pretty sure he poisoned the pilot—he had a seizure and died. The plane is going to crash any minute. The thief wanted me to be blamed for this, but I had nothing to do with it, I promise. He also thought he had the diamonds with him, but I was able to get them out of his pocket and hide them right before he jumped. If you find these, please take them to the police and explain what happened.

I hope I get to see you again, but if not, I will see you in Heaven with Jesus.

Never doubt how much I love you both!

HSJ

Luann's breath came out like whoosh as thoughts and emotions swamped her. She felt like she was riding a roller coaster that had just finished its frantic and terrifying descent. She finally knew what had happened to her father, and even though it was upsetting, it was also comforting to know his love for her and her mother was strong, and his final thoughts were of his family.

He was also innocent. A great weight seemed to have been removed from her shoulders as the doubt and fear suddenly fell away. He wasn't a thief or a terrible criminal. He hadn't thrown away his family for a life of crime and easy living on some foreign soil. He'd had nothing to do with the theft. Although the letter was the only proof of his innocence and would probably never be seen by a judge in a court of law, she believed every word he had written. His dying words were enough to prove his innocence to her, and that was enough. But there was more.

He had loved her.

She couldn't stop returning to that thought—it wrapped around her like a warm, steady flame, offering solace in the midst of her grief. Her hands shook as she handed the shoe, heavy with its final secrets, to Joaquin. Tears streaked her cheeks, and she didn't try to hide them.

"It's finally over," she whispered, her voice barely audible. "I finally know what happened."

Joaquin's gaze softened, filled with an intensity that made her chest flutter. She leaned into him instinctively, letting the weight of her relief—and something more—press against him. His arms wrapped around her without hesitation, strong, steady, protective. She felt the firm pulse of his heart beneath her ear, and for a moment, the rest of the world disappeared.

"Thank you," she murmured into his shoulder, her words trembling. "Thank you for helping me find the truth."

"I'm so glad we know the answers," he replied, his voice low and soothing. "And he was the man you remembered…that must be a comfort."

She tilted her head slightly to meet his eyes, and her breath caught. There was something in Joaquin's gaze—something tender, something searching—that made her heart skip a beat.

"And he was a man of faith," Joaquin continued, his hand brushing a stray strand of hair from her face, his fingers lingering just a heartbeat longer. "I believe his promise. I believe you'll see him again…just like he said."

Her lips curved into a small, grateful smile, but it faltered as her chest swelled with something unspoken. She leaned a little closer, drawn not just by gratitude, but by the quiet warmth radiating from him.

Joaquin's breath mingled with hers, and she could feel the heat of his presence, the steady strength of his arms holding her. Neither moved, yet the air between them seemed to hum with possibility—an unspoken promise hanging there, fragile and new, but thrilling just the same. Neither one knew what the future held, but suddenly, the possibilities were endless.

For a long moment, they simply held each other, the weight of grief melting into something softer, something dangerously tender. And in that silence, she realized a truth she hadn't dared admit: she wasn't alone. God had always been with her, and was also here now, in this moment, helping them both close the doors on the past and consider the future.

"Thank you for reminding me," she whispered. "It is very comforting."

Suddenly Lobo started barking ferociously and Luann heard the click of a pistol being cocked. She and Joaquin turned toward the sound, truly surprised that anyone else was out there in this remote desert location to even witness their discovery. Another truth became glaringly obvious—it had been a mistake to let their guard down at this crucial moment.

"I'll take those diamonds," a rough male voice said from the shadows. "I've been looking for them for years."

Joaquin's hand shot toward his weapon—but the man was faster, and his gun leveled with deadly precision.

"I wouldn't do that, Sheriff," the intruder said, voice low and sharp, each word a warning. "I'm an extremely good shot."

Joaquin froze for a heartbeat, then forced himself to slow his breathing. He couldn't risk a misstep—not with Luann with him. Carefully, he pivoted, sliding her out of the line of fire and moving her gently behind him. Her warm body pressed into his back, trembling, and he felt the rapid beat of her heart against him. Protecting her was everything.

He forced a calm, measured tone, trying to keep the man talking, buying time, feeling every second stretch like a taut wire ready to snap. "Have you been watching us all day?"

The intruder's grin flickered, dangerous and knowing. "Yes, I have. I've been a mile or two behind you ever since you unloaded the horses."

Joaquin's eyes never left the gun, tracing every subtle twitch of the man's shoulders, every flicker of his gaze. He could feel the tension tightening, thick as desert heat. He needed a plan, a split-second opening.

A sudden gust of wind made a nearby branch move and Joaquin's heart leapt at the sound. The gunman also reacted, and his finger twitched on the trigger. A shot rang out and the bullet ripped through the air just inches from Luann's shoulder and ricocheted off some rocks behind her. She gasped, frozen in shock, and Joaquin's pulse thundered in his ears.

"Stay behind me," he ordered, his voice low and for her ears only. He reached behind him, making sure she was staying out of sight. His every muscle was coiled, every sense alive. He could feel the threat like a living thing, circling, waiting. He needed to act—fast—before the next shot found its mark and this criminal succeeded in silencing them both forever.

The intruder's smirk widened, sensing Joaquin's focus, taunting him. But Joaquin held steady, calculating, ready to strike the instant the man faltered. He prayed silently for an opening. He only needed a few seconds. Luann's life—and his own—depended on it.

The man shifted, his chest puffed with the knowledge that he had the upper hand. "I've been doing surveillance ever since that young woman arrived in town asking questions. She just wouldn't stop, no matter what I did to dissuade her." He moved his gun a bit as he talked, but his aim didn't waiver. "I hired people at first, but I learned what I've always known—if you want something done right, you need to do it yourself." His eyes narrowed. "I wondered if you had a copy of Fabio's map, and if so, if you would ever figure out the connection." The criminal took a step closer to the firelight and Joaquin finally got a good look at the man who was pointing a pistol at the two of them. His gut tightened and his mind spun.

It was Carballo, Levi's ranch hand. He was still wearing his work clothes—jeans, heavy boots, a sheepskin jacket and a brown Stetson—but he looked different now. The friendly, easygoing demeanor they'd seen at the barn had been replaced by a steely countenance and dark, evil, hate-filled eyes. This was a murderer who would no doubt kill them both and disappear with the diamonds, leaving more questions than answers behind him.

Joaquin whispered another prayer into the silence of his own mind, clinging to it like a lifeline. *Lord, give me an opening. Something—anything—to protect her.* His palm eased slowly away from the grip of his sidearm, fingers spreading wide in a show of surrender. The motion was deliberate, almost exaggerated, but his every nerve screamed against the restraint. The weight of the Colt on his hip was a constant temptation, a whisper that he could end this in less than a heartbeat—if he moved fast enough. But one wrong twitch would mean a bullet from Carballo's pistol.

The gunman's eyes tracked the shift, cold and flat, a predator sizing up prey. His weapon never wavered, and the faint tic of his trigger finger told Joaquin all he needed to know: the man was itching for a reason to fire.

Sweat trickled down Joaquin's back beneath his shirt, though his voice and face betrayed none of it. He took a careful half step to the side, angling his body even more so Luann was tucked out of the gun's line. He could still feel her just behind him, every shallow breath against his back pressing him harder into his role as shield. Carballo noticed the move, too—his mouth twisting into something between a sneer and a smirk.

"Smart man," the stranger drawled, though his tone held no real praise, only the mockery of a cat letting the mouse believe it had a chance. The barrel of the gun bobbed almost playfully, like a striking snake waiting for the perfect moment.

The air was stifling, charged with the sharp metallic scent of gun oil and the sour tang of sweat. Joaquin's pulse thundered in his ears, but he forced his breathing to remain steady, measured, controlled. He didn't want to die, not here—not now—but more than that, he would not let this madman take Luann's life. Somewhere in the tension, in the endless press of seconds, there had to be a crack he could use.

He just had to survive long enough to find it.

Before he could stop her, Luann suddenly jerked her head around his shoulder. "So, you're the thief!" she exclaimed, her tone both angry and hurt. She tried to move around Joaquin, but he stopped her with his arm. "You're the one who robbed that store and forced my father onto that plane."

She pushed at Joaquin's barrier and took a threatening step toward the older man, but he moved the pistol and once again flexed his finger near the trigger, his expression filled with a mixture of both pride and menace. Joaquin quickly reached out and pulled her back. "Easy," he said softly, hoping to keep the situation from escalating any further.

"Yeah, it was me," Carballo said with a boastful tone. "I was the mastermind behind the whole thing, and I planned it for weeks. Do you know how long it took for me to verify the diamonds were even in the store? That was no small feat," Carballo said, his voice almost wistful as he described the events that led up to the day that happened so long ago. "It was a great plan. After I knew the diamonds' arrival date, I started casing the store, making notes about the owner's lack of security and the employees' movements. The owner wasn't very careful, you see, and I paid the driver at the security company a few extra bucks once he confirmed the delivery. The owner never hired a guard. Can you believe it? But even if he had, it wouldn't have mattered. I was taking those diamonds. Nothing would have stopped me."

"So why take my father?" Luann accused and moved forward again, apparently unmindful of the gun being pointed at her.

Joaquin reached out this time and secured her tightly around the waist, but she struggled in his arms. He tightened his grip, unwilling to let her go and antagonize the shooter any further. She raised her hands as she spoke, and he realized it was futile to subdue her. This confrontation had been building inside her, just waiting to be released. "Why not just rob the place and leave him tied up or something? Why did he have to die?"

Carballo shrugged. "He saw my face," he said nonchalantly. "There was no way to avoid it, and because of that, I had to take him with me. I also needed him to take the blame. I knew exactly where the cameras were located, and the authorities never even knew I was a part of the robbery. Nobody else could identify me. I got away scot-free with no one being the wiser. It was a great plan," he said again, as if still trying to convince himself. "Your father was just collateral damage."

He lowered the gun a tad and paced a bit back and forth. "I had the pilot waiting for me at the airport, and my strategy was always to kill the pilot and jump out of the plane right before it crashed, killing anyone else I had to take with me, your father included. I even procured a special poison for the pilot to make it look like he just had a heart attack. I knew they would do an autopsy and it would look like natural causes. Everything went smoothly." He sneered. "But your father had to be a hero at the last minute and mess up all my plans. He tried to save the pilot, and we got into an all-out brawl. I was able to get away, and I thought I had the diamonds on me, but your father must have gotten them out of my pocket somehow during the fight." He smiled, but it was a malevolent smile. "There weren't any more parachutes, I made sure of that, and the pilot was dead or dying when I jumped. Your dad must have jumped, too, hoping to survive. I guess now we finally know where he ended up." He motioned toward the treetops.

"So, you've been searching for his body all this time?" Joaquin asked.

"Yes. I figured if I could find his body, I could find the diamonds. I knew they'd be together since they weren't found at the crash site, but honestly, I really wasn't sure I would ever find them. I partnered up with Fabio, and he was helping me look. We were both doing a grid search, and over the last twenty years, we've covered almost all of this territory along that plane's flight path. It hasn't been easy."

"So what?" Luann said forcefully, her tone disgusted.

"You want us to feel sorry for you because your plan went amiss and you didn't get to keep your ill-gotten gains?"

Carballo chuckled. "No, little lady, but I do deserve your respect. I am a master criminal, after all. If your father hadn't tried to save that pilot, it all would have gone off without a hitch."

"Why'd you kill Fabio?" Luann asked with a jerk of her body. "It sounds like you were friends." She'd given up fighting against Joaquin's grip, but was still surly and angry, and also apparently unwilling to give the man the deference he was asking for. Joaquin didn't blame her. Carballo's bragging and lack of respect for life turned his stomach.

"Because he was a fool," Carballo admitted with a shrug. "He couldn't keep his mouth shut, and it was just a matter of time before he started telling everyone about the search and the missing diamonds. At first, no one believed him. But when you showed up, asking questions, I knew I had to shut him up fast."

"So, you were the one who tried to burn us alive in Fabio's cabin," Joaquin said quietly, his tone soft and purposefully nonthreatening. He wanted complete confirmation of the man's crimes to verify those he had hired someone to do and those he had done himself.

"Yeah, that was me. I needed to stop you both from asking questions."

"And when that didn't work, you hired someone to shoot at us."

"Didn't do much good though, did it? The guy I hired from Albuquerque ended up in the morgue." He made a sucking sound with his teeth. "You're both still here, causing me problems, but it's probably a good thing the shooter didn't succeed. If he had, I wouldn't be here now, finally getting my hands on those stones." He reached out his free hand. "I'll take those diamonds now."

SEVENTEEN

Joaquin shoved the shoe and the contents into the man's hand but kept his other arm locked protectively around Luann's waist. She was trembling, wild-eyed and filled with a roller coaster of emotions now that she'd finally been able to confront the man who had stolen her father from her so long ago. No way was he letting her go. He was still hoping there was a way to talk Carballo down and de-escalate this situation. "So, who was the shooter?" he asked, stalling, buying seconds. He needed an out—any out—to get Luann back to civilization alive.

"Just some local talent out of Albuquerque," Carballo sneered. "And *talent* is generous. The man couldn't hit the broad side of a barn. I'd never met him before I hired him. He was recommended to me—by someone who obviously didn't realize how inept he really was."

Keep him talking, his inner voice prompted.

"Is Carballo even your real name?" Joaquin pressed.

The older man barked a laugh. "No point in hiding it now. You'll never get a chance to tell anyone. My real name is Collin Drake. Someday there'll be a movie about me. Maybe even a great country song." His teeth flashed in a grin.

"You can't be serious," Luann shot back. Her voice shook, but her words cut. "You're not a legend—you're a thief and a murderer. My father was a good man, and you stole him from us. I was only eight years old when he died. Worse, you left my mom never knowing if he walked out on her or if he was lying dead in a ditch somewhere. That's not just cruel—it's evil."

Drake's eyes narrowed to slits. "Your opinion doesn't matter now, does it? Not when you're about to die." He leveled the pistol, arm steady, the cold glint in his gaze promising murder.

Once again, Joaquin shoved Luann behind him, bracing for the shot, his body the only shield he could offer. Drake's finger tightened on the trigger—

Lobo suddenly appeared out of nowhere and exploded into a frenzy, barking and lunging, teeth bared. The sudden noise and movement snapped Drake's attention for a heartbeat. That small distraction was all Joaquin needed. He drew and fired.

The mountainside cracked with twin gunshots, echoes rolling through the pines. Drake staggered, eyes wide, confusion flashing before life drained from them. A bloom of red spread across his chest. He staggered backward, then toppled, dead before the desert dust swallowed his fall.

Relief never came. Joaquin tried to turn toward Luann, but his body betrayed him. His right arm hung useless. Heat seared through his chest and shoulder—fire tearing him apart from the inside out. He looked down. Blood slicked his shirt, spilling faster than he could process. His knees buckled. The ground rushed up and he collapsed onto his side, the pain consuming him.

Through the haze, he forced his gaze upward. Luann's figure wavered above him, unharmed, framed by the burning orange horizon of the New Mexican sky. She was safe—that was all that mattered.

Darkness closed in. His last thought was how beautiful she looked, outlined against the dying light.

Luann gasped, her breath catching in her throat as her body trembled from head to toe. Adrenaline surged so hard through her chest that it felt like her heart might explode. For one terrifying moment, she stood frozen, locked in the nightmare before her eyes.

Drake—Carballo?—whatever his real name had been, lay sprawled in the dirt, a dark pool spreading beneath him. The smell of gunpowder still hung in the cooling mountain air, sharp and metallic, mixing with the coppery tang of blood. His eyes stared blankly at the sky, lifeless, unseeing.

Was he truly dead?

Her gaze snapped away from the corpse and landed on Joaquin—and the sight nearly shattered her. He lay twisted on the ground, blood flowing freely from his chest and staining the rocky soil. His skin had already begun to pale, lips tinged bluish, every shallow breath a desperate struggle.

"Joaquin," she whispered, dropping to her knees in the New Mexican sand.

She moved on instinct, her hands fumbling as she scooped up both pistols and jammed them into her waistband. Then, with a shuddering breath, she forced herself to lean over Drake and press two fingers to his neck. Nothing. No pulse. No life. He was gone. But Joaquin wasn't—not yet. She moved to his side, her heart beating frantically against her rib cage as she felt for a pulse. He had to survive. He just had to.

She found the beat and a surge of adrenaline swept through her from head to toe. Her hands shook violently as she tore off her jacket and flannel shirt, , then put the jacket back on over her t-shirt to ward off the growing mountain chill. She ripped the flannel-shirt into strips, teeth clenching against the fabric, and pressed the makeshift bandages hard against Joaquin's chest wound. Hot blood seeped through, slicking her fingers and warm against her skin in a way that made her stomach lurch.

"Please, God," she whispered. "Please stop the bleeding."

Her mind spun, grasping for options. She couldn't lose him. He had saved her—he had thrown himself into the line of fire for her. Tears blurred her vision. That kind of selfless love was rare, and the truth of it struck her like lightning: she loved him. She had been too blind, too focused on her own problems, to see it until now. The force of the realization hit so hard she nearly gagged, nausea twisting in her stomach. She loved him, and he was slipping away. Her hands scrambled for her phone. She entered the password. No signal. Not a single bar. A sob tore from her throat as she shoved it back into her pocket.

The horses. They were her only chance.

Her head snapped up. The animals stood tethered to the highline, silhouettes against the fading light, ears flicking nervously at the lingering echo of gunfire. Nearby, saddles lay in a heap where Joaquin had left them. Her chest tightened. The sun was dropping fast; darkness was creeping in from the trees. If she didn't act quickly, she would lose Joaquin forever.

She stumbled to her feet and rushed to the horses, her fingers clumsy and stiff as she threw the saddles over their backs. Every buckle and strap seemed to resist her trembling hands. Her breath came in ragged gasps as she fought the tack into place, muttering frantic prayers with every motion. By the time she dragged Joaquin's horse close, sweat streaked her face and her hands were raw. She dropped to her knees again, brushing her palm across his cheek. His eyes were closed, his breathing shallow and ragged. She shook his shoulder. "Joaquin, please—Wake up. I need your help."

He didn't stir. He was unconscious. And far too heavy for her to move.

Hopelessness slammed into her, stealing her breath. How was she supposed to lift him onto a horse by herself? Fear clawed at her chest, threatening to paralyze her again. The thought of losing him—now, after realizing the depth of her feelings—was unbearable. She squeezed her eyes shut and prayed. *Dear God, please help me. Please show me how to save him.*

An image flickered through her mind—old lessons from history class. The Plains peoples' Travois. She opened her eyes, her pulse pounding. Yes. It could work. It had to. She was no expert, but at least she had a plan.

She scrambled into the trees, yanking down two long saplings and one shorter branch. Her hands flew, binding them into a crude A-frame with rope stripped from the highline. She stretched tent fabric over the frame, shoved sleeping bags on top, then tied the ugly contraption to Joaquin's horse. The animal shifted and tossed its head, unhappy with the weight dragging behind, but she soothed it with shaking hands until it settled and accepted the load.

Now came the hardest part.

She slid her arms beneath Joaquin's shoulders and heaved with everything she had. Nothing. He was like deadweight, impossibly heavy.

"God, please!" she cried out, her voice breaking.

Lobo even dashed forward, teeth gripping Joaquin's jacket, tugging with desperate growls. The dog seemed to know what was required, and was doing his best to help, all to no avail. Then suddenly, for one heart-stopping moment, Joaquin groaned—just enough to shift his body. With Luann pulling, the dog straining, and Joaquin's last flicker of strength, they managed to drag him onto the travois.

Luann's breath came in sobs as she lashed him down with the last of the rope, whispering shaky reassurances. She checked his wounds again. Blood still seeped, but it was much slower now. His forehead glistened with sweat, his face pale as ash. His lips were drawn tight with pain, even in unconsciousness.

She had to move. Now.

She kicked dirt over the fire, mounted her horse, tied Joaquin's reins to her saddle horn, and switched on her phone's flashlight. A narrow beam cut through the night, illuminating only a few feet ahead. With a final glance at the corpse she'd left behind, Luann turned the horses toward the truck. Every jolt made her wince, imagining the agony it was causing Joaquin. Her eyes darted constantly between the rough ground and the useless phone screen, praying for a single bar of service to appear.

The diamonds and her father's note pressed heavily against her chest from the pocket of her jacket. Behind her lay Drake's body, cooling in the dirt. Ahead stretched miles of darkness and uncertainty. Luann gripped the reins tight. Every step the horses took, she whispered a prayer. For strength. For light. For Joaquin's life.

EIGHTEEN

Joaquin groaned; a low, ragged sound that ripped from his chest. Pain lanced through him with every shallow breath, not just in his chest, but down his back, his legs, everywhere that his body had bumped as the travois had carried him across the rocky mountainside. He had little memory of the trip—just bits and pieces that flickered in his mind. His eyes fluttered open, squinting against the blinding white of the room. Sterile walls, harsh fluorescent lights, the sharp antiseptic scent filling his nose. *Hospital? How...?*

Memories crashed against him in fragments. Carballo's smirk, the crack of gunfire, the desert wind whipping through the canyon, Luann's scream. His chest tightened with the memory of the blood on the rocks, the taste of iron in the air, the terror of losing her. She had to be safe—she *was* safe, right? His stomach twisted, panic rising.

A soft pressure on his hand pulled him back, grounding him in the present. And then her lips, light as gossamer, brushed against his forehead. Warm, trembling hands cupped his face. Tears glittered in her eyes, catching the harsh light like tiny, fragile stars.

"Oh, I can't believe it," she whispered, voice breaking. "God really is good, all the time. I thought… I thought you were going to die. You lost so much blood…"

The ache in his chest mingled with relief so sharp it took his breath away. She was alive. *They* were alive. Somehow. And there she was, real and warm and alive, pressing her lips against him. The weight of that realization made him dizzy with gratitude and wonder.

Before he could speak, a tall figure appeared—a doctor in a crisp white coat, iPad in hand. She moved with calm precision though her eyes flicked to him with concern.

"Well, hello, Sheriff Fuentes. I'm very pleased to see you awake."

Joaquin blinked several times, trying to place her. Pain stabbed through his chest, sharp and insistent. "Where… am I? How…?" His voice was hoarse, each word a struggle. "I hurt."

"I imagine you do," she said gently, checking the monitors that tracked his every pulse and breath. "You've just come out of surgery. Everything looks good. With physical therapy and time, I expect a full recovery."

"Recovery from…what?" His mind scrambled, pulling at the jagged threads of memory that kept returning in bits and pieces: the scent of gunpowder, Luann screaming, the cold, unyielding mountain rocks beneath him, Drake—Carballo—falling.

"Carballo shot you at the same time you shot him," Luann said softly, her hand still resting on his. "You were the better shot. He's dead. You got hit in the chest."

The doctor's gaze hardened slightly. "A half inch to the left, and you wouldn't be here. We had to repair significant damage, and you lost a great deal of blood. You owe your life to this lady here," she said, motioning to Luann.

Joaquin's chest tightened again. "Really? I… I don't remember. How?"

The doctor smiled faintly. "She rigged a travois and used the horses to pull you out of the wilderness until she could get a signal on her phone and call for help. Your deputy called in the Life Flight helicopter. Without her, you would have bled out before help could have reached you."

Pain flared anew, sharp and relentless. He clenched his teeth, struggling to hold still. "I…really hurt," he whispered, the words tasting of blood and iron. Every attempt to remember the events only twisted the pain sharper.

"Are you staying with him?" the doctor asked.

"I am," Luann said without hesitation.

"He'll probably fall asleep again—that's good. He needs rest." She checked something else on her iPad, then gave a gentle smile. "The nurses are monitoring his condition, but if you have any concerns, give them a buzz with this red button. Okay?"

"Got it," Luann replied, her fingers entwined with Joaquin's, her thumb brushing his clammy skin.

Joaquin tried to focus on their words, but the effort made his head spin. The fluorescent lights blurred into white streaks, shadows melting into corners. Memories of the mountainside—dust swirling in the wind, the metallic tang of blood, Lobo's growl—continued to press against the edges of his mind. Panic and relief collided, sharp and confusing.

Gradually, the world softened. Darkness crept back at the edges of his vision, but the pain dulled, replaced with the warmth of Luann leaning close, the steady, grounding pressure of her hand on his arm. He let himself drift, carried between consciousness and sleep, the hum of machines and her gentle presence tethering him to life.

Even as blackness swallowed him again, he felt it: alive, safe and loved.

"Joaquin?"

Luann leaned over him, the warm washcloth pressed to his brow, damp with the faint scent of antiseptic. His eyes fluttered open, sluggish and heavy, and for a moment she held her breath, willing him to see her, to recognize her in the sterile haze of the hospital room. Forty-eight hours of nearly total unconsciousness had left her unsure what he had experienced, and what fragments of the nightmare he'd absorbed and remembered.

Outside the room, faint sounds drifted in—curious deputies, neighbors, the low hum of hospital machinery—but Luann blocked them out. The bed-and-breakfast owners were keeping Camila safely away, shielding her from the grisly aftermath of the shooting. The little girl wasn't ready to see her father in this fragile, broken state, but once he was strong enough, Luann was determined to bring her by so she could be reassured and Joaquin could be buoyed by her presence.

Joaquin's law enforcement team had been overwhelmed but had still acted professionally while working through their duties, even without their fearless leader at the helm. Once Joaquin's vitals stabilized, Ricky had interrogated Luann right there in the room and sent his report up the chain. As a result, the FBI had swooped in, their presence making the hospital feel like a tactical command center. Agents moved through the halls, crisp suits brushing against gurneys, their radios clicking and murmuring in low tones. The diamonds, once in her father's old shoe, were now in FBI custody along with her father's note. Luann had handed them over without hesitation, and was glad to finally prove his innocence, once and for all. Now that her father's fate had been discovered, she was ready to put the violence and death and the entire episode behind her.

The bodies had been recovered—both her father's and Collin Drake's—and now Del Norte and nearby Tijeras were flooded with reporters, cameras flashing like distant gunfire, voices scraping through the town like static at every restaurant and small shop along the thoroughfare. She'd ignored them all as she'd returned to the bed-and-breakfast to gather her things and then come back to the hospital, calling her mother along the way. She'd shared the truth about everything they had discovered, and for a brief, fragile moment, her mother's terminal illness seemed lighter, almost bearable. They had cried together, shared their joy and sadness, and begun the process of planning the funeral for the man who had given everything he had to protect them.

Now, all of Luann's energy centered on Joaquin. She owed him everything. Life. Clarity. The knowledge that they were alive to fight another day. She set aside the washcloth, watching the shallow rise and fall of his chest, the quiet hum of the oxygen machine punctuating the room's tense stillness. Sleep claimed him again almost immediately, as the doctor had warned, and she returned to the chair, curling into it with the wonderful romance novel she had grabbed from the gift shop.

A dry whisper broke the silence. "Thirsty."

Her heart leapt. "You're awake!" Relief surged, sharp and vivid. She grabbed a cup with a bendy straw and poured water from the pitcher, then guided it to his lips. He sipped slowly, each movement deliberate, tentative, and the silence that followed felt like a suspended heartbeat.

"Have you been here long?" His voice was a rasp, fragile as smoke.

"A few days," she whispered, careful not to let the urgency creep in. "I went and got my suitcase from the bed-and-breakfast so I could take care of you. Too bad there's no laundry service here. I may have to slip out in a day or so and do a load." She managed a small tired smile. "How are you feeling?"

"Better," he said, voice rough but steady. "Camila?"

"She's safe." Luann tucked a loose strand of hair behind her ear. "Susanna and Ted are watching her. They didn't want to worry her by letting her see you unconscious, so they've been keeping her at the bed-and-breakfast. When you're ready, either I'll bring her over or they will. Lobo's fine, too—Ricky's taking care of him until you're able to come home."

"Good plan." His fingers found hers. The tremor in his hand betrayed the effort of even that small motion. She squeezed back, and soon they were holding hands, his thumb tracing slow, deliberate circles over the back of her hand—a grounding ritual in the quiet storm of the hospital.

"You didn't leave," he murmured, eyes searching hers.

"I love you," she said, steady despite the adrenaline still thrumming through her veins. "I know...you might not feel the same…" She hesitated, swallowing the fear that had been clawing at her throat. "But I couldn't leave you by yourself. I had to stay to make sure you were okay."

"I love you back." His words cut through the air, urgent, insistent. "I don't want you going back to Clovis. Stay. Please."

Her lips trembled as she leaned forward, pressing a soft, deliberate kiss to his, a kiss that tasted of relief, promise and survival. "I'll stay," she whispered, letting the words solidify the fragile victory they had clawed from the brink of disaster. For the first time in days, she allowed herself to breathe.

EPILOGUE

Two months later

Luann stood at the edge of the gravel drive in front of the bed-and-breakfast, the crisp winter wind brushing strands of hair against her cheeks as the car pulled to a stop. Luann felt her throat tighten as the door opened and her mother stepped out—frail, thinner than she remembered, but smiling with a light that hadn't dimmed. "Mom," she whispered, before her legs carried her the rest of the way. She wrapped her arms around the woman who had been both anchor and compass, inhaling the faint scent of lavender lotion mixed with the antiseptic trace of hospitals. For a moment, Luann wished she could hold her mother forever, as if love could stop the steady march of time or disease.

Her mother leaned back, studying her daughter's face. "You look different," she said softly. "Happier. Stronger."

Luann's smile trembled. "I am both." She turned slightly, motioning to where Joaquin stood near the porch steps, Camila at his side with a wide, toothy grin, and Lobo wagging his tail as if he, too, understood the magnitude of introductions and the excitement of the moment.

"Mom," Luann said, drawing a breath, "This is Joaquin and his daughter, Camila. And this scruffy guy is Lobo, the most wonderful dog you'll ever meet." Joaquin had still been in the hospital when Henry St. John's funeral had occurred, and once released, his time had been filled with therapy and follow-up medical appointments to make sure his recovery was strong and on track. He hadn't had a chance to meet Theresa St. John before today, except briefly through a Zoom call or two over the internet.

After the burial, Theresa had suffered through a medical setback and had been hospitalized on and off for the last two months. She was only now feeling strong enough to drive again but had insisted on coming to Del Norte to get to know Joaquin and Camila and see the little town. Luann was delighted that they could finally meet each other in person, here in Del Norte.

Her mother's eyes warmed as she extended a hand, though Joaquin stepped forward and gently enclosed it in both of his. "It's an honor to see you," he said, his voice steady, carrying the weight of a man who had lived through danger and loss but still chose love.

"The honor's mine," her mother replied, studying him. "I can see why she smiles differently now." She smiled. "Thank you again for saving my daughter's life, and for everything you did to help her discover what happened to my Henry. Words can never be enough to express my gratitude."

Camila shyly presented a small bouquet of wildflowers she had picked that morning, and Lobo pressed his head against Luann's mother's leg as though sealing the welcome. The moment was simple, ordinary in its domesticity—but to Luann, it felt like a miracle carved out of the chaos of the past few months. They were all here, together. She said a quick prayer of thanksgiving, knowing that God had made this moment possible.

That evening, Susanna cooked them a hearty dinner and then discreetly disappeared with Ted, leaving the small group in the living room with time to themselves. There were no other tenants currently renting a room at the small B and B, and the private group enjoyed several hours of stories, laughter and quiet pauses. Luann and Joaquin eventually made their way over to the mantel, where they stood together in the glow and warmth of the fire. Camila had fallen asleep on the couch, her head resting against Luann's mother's lap, while Lobo sprawled nearby, paws twitching in dreams of chasing rabbits and roadrunners.

Joaquin took Luann's hand, fingers interlacing with hers. "We should tell her," he murmured.

Luann's heart fluttered. She nodded, and together they turned toward the woman who had always been her fiercest advocate.

"Mom," Luann began, her voice soft but clear. "There's something we'd like to share with you."

Her mother's eyes twinkled knowingly. "Something tells me you're not coming back to live in Clovis."

Luann laughed, the sound bubbling up like a release of tension. She had made several trips back and forth between Del Norte and Clovis as she'd tried to make sure her mother's needs were met during her medical crisis, and Joaquin's were met as he healed from his gunshot wound. But now that Theresa's condition had stabilized, at least for the time being, and Joaquin was on the mend, she'd had a chance to make plans for her own life. The time had been well spent, and she and Joaquin had been able to spend a lot of quality time together when she was in Del Norte. The more she knew about Joaquin, the more she loved this quiet, gentle man. She couldn't keep their secret a moment longer. With a smile, she winked at her mom. "You're right, and we are engaged." She held out her hand, and the simple elegant ring caught the firelight.

Tears shimmered in her mother's eyes, but her smile widened. "Oh, sweetheart. I'm thrilled for you." Her gaze shifted to Joaquin. "Take care of her, Joaquin. She is a really special girl."

"I intend to," Joaquin replied, his voice solemn but filled with conviction. "And I totally agree."

Luann smiled at her fiancé, filled with love and excitement about the future. Even though he'd been dealing with his own health issues and recovery, he had kept her apprised of the FBI's progress as they'd investigated Drake's history and eventually closed the case. Several newspapers and bloggers had published stories about the crash and the showdown in the desert, and Luann had even been approached by an agent, asking if she would be willing to write a novel from her father's point of view. Luann was still considering it.

The weeks that followed were a whirlwind of change. Luann's mother, after careful discussions with her doctors, made the decision to move into a residential cancer treatment center in Albuquerque. The facility was well regarded, with advanced therapies and a compassionate staff. More importantly, it was only a short drive from Del Norte, placing her within a few minutes' reach of Luann's new life.

Luann spent the first morning touring the center with her mother, noticing the sunlit courtyards, the library stocked with books and the soft music that seemed to float through the halls. Though part of her rebelled at the idea of her mother needing such a place, she also felt a quiet relief knowing that care and comfort were within reach.

"It's not home," her mother admitted, looking out the window at a stand of cottonwoods, their golden leaves quivering in the breeze. "But it's close enough. And I'll be closer to you."

Luann squeezed her hand. "That's all I want."

While her mother settled in, Luann began her own new chapter. She rented a small carriage house in Tijeras, since there wasn't anything available in Del Norte, and submitted applications to schools across the Albuquerque area, determined to root herself in a place where she could balance her roles as daughter, teacher and soon-to-be wife. When the University of New Mexico called to schedule an interview, Luann felt a spark of destiny. She prepared meticulously, polishing her résumé and rehearsing her responses late into the night. Joaquin quizzed her with mock interview questions, and Camila sat nearby offering encouragement, occasionally chiming in with suggestions that made them all laugh.

On the afternoon of the interview, Luann stood before the mirror, smoothing the fabric of her navy dress. Her nerves trembled beneath her calm exterior, but when Joaquin kissed her forehead and whispered, "You've got this," the fear shifted into resolve.

The university's campus was sprawling, filled with adobe-style buildings that reflected both tradition and innovation. As Luann walked through the halls, she imagined herself lecturing in classrooms, guiding students through literature and language studies, and weaving her passion for teaching into the next generation. By the time she left the interview, her chest felt lighter, her steps quicker. For the first time in years, she could see her future unfolding with clarity.

In the midst of professional ambitions and personal transitions, faith became a steadying rhythm. Luann and Joaquin attended church together whenever possible, their hands entwined during prayers, their voices rising in songs of worship. Neither of them had been untouched by abandonment—Luann through her father's absence, Joaquin through loss and betrayal—but together they began to rebuild trust, forming a new family from the broken remnants of the past.

One Sunday morning, as sunlight streamed through stained-glass windows, Joaquin glanced at Luann and found her already looking at him. The quiet strength in her eyes reminded him that healing was not an individual pursuit but a shared journey. He said a silent prayer of gratitude. God had brought this lovely lady into his life, taught him that second chances were real and helped heal his wounded heart. Once the service concluded, they walked hand in hand across the churchyard to pick up Camila from her Sunday School class. "I used to think faith meant never doubting," he said quietly. "But I think now it means choosing to trust, even when doubt whispers louder."

Luann nodded. "I agree," she whispered, and then kissed him, right there by the corner of the building. "I love you, you know."

"I love you back." He smiled. They squeezed each other's hands, a silent vow forming long before the official one. He drew his hand gently down her cheek, his heart filled with awe and certainty. He had a new beginning, one that was the culmination of survival, of trust reclaimed and of love reborn.

* * * * *

If you liked this story from Kathleen Tailer, check out her previous Love Inspired Suspense books:

Surviving the Desert
Showdown in the Rockies
Marked to Die

Available now from Love Inspired Suspense!

Find more great reads at www.LoveInspired.com.

Dear Reader,

The themes of love, trust and healing you encounter in this book are not just stories; they are deeply rooted in the struggles that many of us face in our own lives, especially when it comes to abandonment.

Abandonment, in any form, can leave wounds that are hard to heal. Whether it's the abandonment of a parent, a spouse, a friend or even feeling deserted by God in moments of hardship, the pain of being left behind can leave scars that seem insurmountable.

It's easy to feel isolated when faced with loss. We ask, *How could this happen to me?* or *Why did they leave me when I needed them the most?* It's in these moments of pain that God gently whispers to us, reminding us of His unfailing love and presence. The Bible assures us time and again that He will never leave us or forsake us (Deuteronomy 31:6, Hebrews 13:5). He is the ultimate source of healing and restoration, even when we can't see the path forward.

I pray that, through the unfolding drama and romance in this book, you find a renewed sense of hope and trust in the God who sees you, loves you and will never abandon you.

With love and grace,
Kathleen Tailer